my
canvas
bag

LUCAS KINKAID

ISBN 979-8-9856899-1-4 (Print Book Paperback)
ISBN 979-8-9856899-2-1 (Print Book Hardback)
ISBN 979-8-9856899-3-8 (eBook)

DEDICATION

This book is dedicated to all who struggle
to overcome a painful past.

CONTENTS

FROM THE AUTHOR

Many people are born into a bad family situation. Loneliness, frustration, and anger can build. This can result in giving up and making bad decisions. Once hope for tomorrow is lost, today and what happens in it, no longer matter.

There comes a time when a path must be chosen. Those who choose negativity and despair go on a journey into hell. This is easy. The struggle comes when choosing a path away from bad things. It means facing judgment from others who can't understand or relate to a dysfunctional family. This is a journey of accepting reality and working to discover the good inside.

Choosing a path away from the bad is difficult. It is also worth it.

CHAPTER 1

A Rather Good Day

It is autumn and I'm standing at a window in my bedroom looking at the long pasture in front of our house. The sun is rising slowly. The light of the day is getting stronger and brighter. Leaves that have served their purpose during the summer months are now hanging like old, wrinkled ornaments on trees. As I look outside, I soon realize that leaves don't get to determine their final resting place in this world. It's the wind that makes this decision. The wind will sweep dead leaves from tree limbs or gutters and make them move across roads or dance in the air. The wind will then choose where the leaves should be to start the process of turning into soil. The land seems like the wind's canvas and the leaves are its paints.

The year is 1970, and I am an eleven-year-old boy looking forward to the day. My friend John calls my house the night before. He tells me he'd like me to come to his house and play with the new cars and plastic race tracks he has gotten for his birthday. We set a time and I tell him I will be there. During our phone call, John asks if it is okay with my parents. I tell him they said it would be fine.

I didn't dare mention the reality of what is happening. After John hangs up, I go into the kitchen. My mother is there in one of her phases of drinking. She always sits in a chair at the kitchen table with her beer in a small glass and a can of beer next to it. The ashtray on the kitchen table is usually full. Holding her cigarette in one hand, she has her other hand cradled around her glass of beer. I ask if I can go to my friend John's house the next day. She is annoyed with my question and seems to ignore me. After she looks away, I ask a second time. I hear the sigh and the look of anger on her face as she carefully places the ashes from her current cigarette into the ashtray with all the other used ones.

"Whatever. You're just like your father. You're going to do what you want no matter how it affects anyone."

My half-sister is at the table and motions for me to leave. I take my mother's response as telling me it is okay. My half-sister is five years older than me and knows how to handle my mother's drunken episodes. She's been doing it much longer than me.

I get dressed and make myself some toast for breakfast and have a big glass of milk. I go outside and get my orange bike. This is an object of my pride. I love my bike. It is known as a banana bike with its high handlebars and long seat. I ride it daily until the weather stops me.

Using my bike to get to John's house will take me some time. I estimate over an hour or more of riding. I know shortcuts through the woods and I take them all. I then ride on the road for a long time. I can see my breath and the frost on the grass as I ride. The day's temperature is slowly getting warmer. It's early enough in the day that there are very few cars on these rural roads. I'm to be there at 11 a.m., and I should be on time.

I eventually see John's house and I'm tired. He has a steep driveway. It's too much to ride up with a single-gear bike. I walk my bike up the hill. When I get there, it is only a few minutes after 11 a.m. I started at 9:30 and actually enjoyed the ride.

I ring the doorbell and when the door opens, it's John's mother. She has a bright smile.

She says, "You must be Mark. Please come in. Did your parents have any problem finding our house?"

It is happening again. Another situation where I have to hide the truth. I'm holding a bike, but John's mother assumes my parents drove me here. I know if I say my parents were up late last night drinking and are sleeping late today, it would not be received well. I can't tell them my father is going somewhere to be with his buddies today and my mother doesn't get up until around noon after a night like last night. I'd get that shocked and surprised look. I'd then be labeled as someone who is to be avoided. So, I make up a quick lie.

"Well, my dad had to go visit a friend near here. I just rode up from there."

When she asks where, I tell her another lie. I mention a house where my half-sister's friend lives. John's mother smiles, but I know my story doesn't make any sense to her. I don't care. I'm going to have fun.

I'm instructed to go to the finished basement of their home. It is a fun place filled with toys and games. Plastic tracks are set up and John has his many cars carefully placed beside the plastic tracks. We are having a great time. I hear someone coming down the steps, and it's John's mother. She has brought us a snack of potato chips and Kool-Aid. I am having the best possible time.

I use their downstairs bathroom. When I'm done, I open the bathroom door and see something that always amazes me. John's mother leans down and gently nuzzles her head against his and hugs him. She then tells John she loves him. John smiles and tells his mom he loves her too.

I've seen things like this before. I can't imagine something like this happening to me. I've always been very scared of my mother. When she drinks, she is unpredictable with her anger. When she's sober, I'm not to bother her. For a few seconds, I let my mind think about what John must be feeling. The happiness of not being afraid of your mother. I think it must be pleasant. I feel bad for myself, but I smile. I'm having a good time.

John's mother invites me to stay for lunch, and I eagerly agree. They have chicken noodle soup with sandwiches. John's mother made the bread earlier that morning. Everything is delicious. After lunch, John and I go outside and toss around a football. It is such a nice day. I look to the side and see John's father come up to me.

"Glad to have you here, Mark. We have to do some shopping today. Can I call your parents to come and get you?"

There it is again. That nervous feeling inside my stomach. I can't tell them the truth. We've had such a nice time. I have no idea where my father is and my mother doesn't drive. They'll think bad things of me if I tell them I'm going to ride my bike all the way home.

"I'll probably just ride to the closed golf course. I have a cousin who lives near there."

I know John's father doesn't believe me. His wife comes out, and they turn away and have a conversation. When they turn back, they are both smiling.

"Hey, how about I load your bike into our station wagon and drive you home? Would that be, okay?"

I try to tell them I can ride my bike to my fictitious cousin's home, but they eventually get me to agree to have me and my bike driven home.

When we get to my house, I thank them. John's father gets my bike from the back of his station wagon. He asks if I'm sure someone is home. I tell him my mother is home. I thank them again and walk as fast as I can with my bike to the back porch and carefully put it in its spot. I don't move until I see their car going down the road. I know John's father likes me. He probably wants to meet my parents and get to know them. How do I tell John's father I can't risk him meeting my mother? I don't know if she has been drinking and what phase of drunkenness she is in right now. She may say crazy and embarrassing things. It's better to just wait until they're gone.

As I sit on the back porch, I realize John's parents know things about me without me saying a word. I can sense they have the impression that something is not right with my family. They're new here. They'll eventually hear the stories about my mother and father. The stories about the police being called to our house. My mother drinking too much and being kicked out of bars for fighting. Then they'll avoid me. Everybody eventually does. I'm still happy thinking that at least I had a great day today.

I make it inside and suddenly realize my day is now going to become bad. My mother is sitting at the kitchen table with a can of beer in front of her and holding the glass full of foamy yellow brew with both of her hands. The house has been completely cleaned. My mother seems to believe that everything is okay if you have a clean house. I ask where my father is, and she gives the standard response of not knowing and not caring. I then ask where my half-sister is. My mother informs me she went with some girlfriends to do some shopping. This is bad. It means I must sit at the kitchen table with my mother as she drinks. I've tried to avoid this in the past. If I try to leave and watch television, she'll turn it off and lecture me about being a thankless son. I'll hear how I'm like my father and have no respect for women. If I go anywhere in the house, she'll follow me. If I try to leave, she'll start calling people. Then other kids and parents will come looking for me. It is something that's happened before. I resign myself to the fact that I must sit there and listen to drunken ranting.

When my mother is drinking, she regularly tells me how much she hates my father and dislikes me. I am going to have to listen to how she regrets having me, and I'm the only reason she puts up with my father. Without me, she would be free. I'll also hear that a child as awful as I am should be thankful to have a mother willing to sacrifice herself by putting up with my father. I'm just thankless like my father.

This is easy to hear compared to her advanced stages of drunkenness. That is when she can get angry and, for no reason, will throw things. The night before I had to clean up a wine bottle she had thrown after my father poured the remaining amount of wine down the kitchen sink. The bottle shattered and it took me a while to get all the pieces of glass cleaned up.

I have been listening to my mother's drunken rants for about three hours when my half-sister arrives home. She asks to see me in another room. Like one night watchman talking to the other, I inform her of how much beer our mother has had so far today. I tell her about our mother's mood and what she has been talking about. My half-sister informs me that my father is at his veterans club and drinking with his buddies.

It isn't going to be an easy night. When those two are both drinking, it can become something terrible. Our house has been trashed more than once and the police have been called to break up their fights. It is going to be a stressful evening.

My half-sister takes over my spot sitting at the kitchen table with my mother. I'm now free to leave. Her goal will be to try to talk my mother into getting something to eat and then get her to bed before my father arrives home. If this can happen, chaos can be avoided. My half-sister knows how to make this happen much better than I do.

It's dark outside, but I open up the front door and leave. I go to a stone building not far from our house. It was built when the property around the house was a farm. I use the light from the moon to find my way there and get my canvas bag. I open it up and pull out a flashlight. I use this to make my way into the nearby woods.

It's getting cold. The leaves crunch as I carefully move around trees. I hear an owl making his hooting sound as I enter the woods. It's as if the owl is announcing my arrival. I find my usual spot among the trees and get set up. I put a wool blanket down on the ground to lay on and have a down-filled blanket to place around me. I pull books out of my canvas bag. They are about baseball, and I also have magazines about baseball. There are some cans of food. Tonight's dinner will be a can of corn and a can of baked beans. I also have a tin canteen filled with water. My pocket knife has a can opener in it, and I quickly put it to good use. I use the spoon that is also part of the pocket knife. When I'm finished, I put the empty cans next to a tree stump about eight feet away. I eventually hear a rustle of leaves and know he's arrived. It's an opossum. I've named him Larry. He goes and licks out what is left in the cans. We started this ritual of the empty cans next to the tree stump a few months ago. I shine the flashlight on him, and he doesn't run. If he could talk, I believe Larry the opossum would tell me to stop shining the light on him as he's eating.

I turn off the flashlight and look at my house. My parents have never slept in the same bedroom since I've been alive. There is a light on in my father's bedroom. He's home and the rest of the house is quiet. My half-sister must have gotten my mother to eat and go to bed before he got home. She is amazing in that way.

I love the peace and quiet of the woods. I enjoy the freedom of being able to do what I want without the need for approval. I don't feel forced to lie or worry about the judgments of others. I'm free of my mother's drunken rants and my parents' fighting. The night air is cool and crisp. I'm warm and happy among my blankets and baseball literature.

Since it appears the police won't have to be called and the house isn't going to be trashed, it is finally time to relax. I fall asleep. I wake up when I hear some deer snorting at me. According to my watch, it is 2 a.m. I decide to place my things back into the canvas bag and put it back in the stone house. I gather the cans that the opossum Larry had cleaned out and toss them in the outside trash can when I get to the house.

I check the front door and it's locked. I check the back door and it's locked. I go to the basement door and it's open. I always make sure it is unlocked before I leave to go to the woods.

I'm very quiet as I go through the house to my bedroom. I get my clothes off and climb into bed. I know what's going to happen with John. He'll be told about me and my family by the other kids in school. I'll never be invited to his house again. He'll start to ignore me and then will treat me as if I don't exist like the other kids. It's happened before. When I think about it, for me, it doesn't matter. I've still had a rather good day.

CHAPTER 2

A Time of Change

Spring has finally arrived. This is an exciting time in my life. School is going to be over in a few days. My twelfth birthday is over the summer. It will soon be baseball season. This is the last year I can play in Little League, and I can't wait to start. When not involved with practice or a game, I will play baseball with other kids in pick-up games. I love playing baseball. I can do it all day every day and never get tired of it. My bedroom is filled with baseball cards, baseball magazines, as well as books about baseball. Pictures of baseball players are on my wall. I anticipate a great summer.

I learned at a young age that life always changes and that nothing ever stays the same. Some changes can be gradual. I remember growing and my favorite shoes getting too small and being able to ride a bike after trying for many days. Other things can be unexpected and forever change your life.

When I was nine years old, my father got me a dog. I loved the dog. It was a female and I named her Wendy after the comic character Wendy the Witch. We had a great time playing in the yard. She would sleep with me, and I couldn't wait to see her after I got out of school.

One day I get home after school and Wendy is gone. I ask my mother where Wendy is. She tells me she hated the dog. It left a dog smell in the house, and she got tired of doing extra cleaning because of a dog. My mother says they had to get rid of the dog mostly because it attacked her.

Wendy didn't attack her. My mother was angry at me because I didn't do something, and she grabbed me and started screaming at me. Wendy went crazy with barking. She even growled at my mother, who then let me go. This made me love Wendy even more. For the first time in my life, I had a protector.

Tears fill my eyes when I realize my Wendy is gone. This makes my mother angry. She screams at me that it was just a dog. She yells it is time I grow up and quit acting like a baby about things.

"I hate you," I scream and run to my room. My mother lets me know she feels the same way about me.

I cry for a long time. I am not called to come down for dinner. My mother doesn't bother me. She tells my father and half-sister that I have been bad and needed to be in my room. It takes a few weeks for me to get over the loss of Wendy. It makes me realize how my life can change instantly in ways I never thought possible.

It is about a month earlier when a kid in school named Billy tries to bully me. He's been doing it for years. I usually try to get away from him or yell for a teacher.

After a tough night with my mother's drinking and my parents' fighting, I am tired and in a very bad mood. My grades are poor because I can't study at my house. My parents care more about their beer and cigarettes than my schoolwork. I've always been considered by other kids to be dumb and the teachers have labeled me as slow.

I'm talking to another kid about our favorite baseball players when Billy comes up and says, "Hey, Cinderella, shut up, I don't want to hear about baseball. I hate that game."

Normally, I'd just be quiet and walk away. Today, I feel different. I have nothing but a miserable home to go back to and a mother who could be crazy drunk when I get there. I feel I have nothing good in my life. I'm not like Billy and the other kids. I feel intense anger and then something inside me snaps. I look at Billy and yell, "Make me."

This is the official challenge to fight in our world. The other kids make their sounds as Billy turns to them and smiles. When he turns back, Billy yells, "I'm going to kick your ass."

Before he says the last word, I'm on him. We're wrestling around with one another and I hit him a few times. He gets behind me and begins hitting me in the head. It's a struggle, but I get turned around. Suddenly, we're exchanging punches like prizefighters. Billy goes to grab me around the middle but I grab his hair, pull his head back, and he lets go.

At this moment, I cannot hear any sounds. I know of nothing going on around me. I can't feel anything. My entire mind is focused on inflicting pain on Billy. I'm in a world I've never known before.

We wrestle around some more and I get him in a headlock. I start hitting him again and again. He's a strong kid and lifts me off of the ground. I keep holding on. He's struggling and punching me on the side and back, but I won't let go.

Then next thing I know, someone is hitting me in the head. I quickly realize somebody is trying to break up the fight. I have no control over myself. I let Billy go and don't realize I'm hitting our school janitor. He hits me back, so I charge him and knock him down like we were playing football.

Then I can't move my arms. Two teachers are holding my arms and pulling me away from the janitor. They are yelling and screaming something at me. I have no idea what they are saying. I slowly look around. I'm surrounded by teachers. There are also teachers around Billy. His face is bloody. I feel something on my lip. I realize my mouth and nose are bleeding. As my breathing starts going back to normal, I begin to feel pain. My head, back, and sides hurt. There is pain all over my face.

A male teacher grabs me by the back of my shirt and drags me away. We pass Billy who has teachers asking him again and again if he is okay. I am taken to the principal's office and placed in a chair. A few tissues are tossed on my lap for my bloody face.

This has never happened to me before. I have never been in trouble. I guess I should be scared, but I am not. I feel good. The fear and anxiety of going home are gone. I have no idea why. I'm thinking they can't do anything worse to me than going home to my drunk mother. I experience a few seconds of feeling invincible.

A teacher comes into the room and speaks into the principal's ear. She then stands behind him, looking at me with an angry expression. I keep thinking to myself how my mother gives me much worse angry looks. I don't know why, but I feel like laughing.

The principal tells me they have spoken to the other kids and it is clear I started the fight.

I scream, "They're lying! He's the one who told me to shut up and when I told him to make me, he started the fight."

The principal and teacher look at one another and smile. The principal lets out a sigh.

"Billy is an excellent student and has never given us any trouble. I imagine you know about his family."

Everyone knows about Billy's family. His father has been on the school board. They own the local auto repair shop in town. Yeah, I know and everybody knows about Billy and his family. Everyone seems to want to ignore how Billy pushes kids around every day.

"So, what's that got to do with the fight?" I ask.

I realize it's happening to me again. Nobody cares about the truth. All they know is the time my mother showed up to a school event drunk and was asked to leave. My father has never been to one of my school events. Everybody knows about my parents' fights and the police being called to break them up. I begin to get really angry. I realize I'm not being punished because of the fight; I'm being punished because of my parents. Am I supposed to accept that Billy can get away with his lies because of his family? The world makes less and less sense to me. I feel my anger returning.

"I'm going to call your mother and tell her what happened. I expect you to go into the next room and apologize to Billy."

"Never," I scream.

"Then you leave me no choice. You will have to get three swats and be suspended for three days. This will be on your permanent record. All of that can be avoided if you simply take responsibility for your actions and apologize."

My fists are tight and my bloody lips are curled. I am furious as I say in a low voice, "I didn't start the fight. I'm not going to apologize. I'm glad I finally got a chance to beat him."

The principal doesn't respond and quickly stands up. He gets his paddle hanging on the wall. I am not afraid. I want to rush him and start hitting him. I know it is best for me to now just take my punishment.

The first swat hurts, and the second one really hurts. I groan a bit after the third swat. I stand up and fight back my tears of rage. The lady teacher is smiling for some reason. I think she enjoys watching me get paddled.

The principal puts the paddle away and says, "Now go to the bathroom and clean yourself up. I'm going to call your mother. I don't want any trouble with you when you wait for the bus or ever again. Do you understand?"

Something new happens as I wait for the bus home that day. The other kids don't talk to me, and when I look at one of them, I see fear in his eyes. As we are getting on the bus, I hear someone say, "That's him over there. He is the guy who got into a fight with Billy and the janitor. Stay away from him. He's crazy."

I get off the bus and walk to my house knowing I'm different. Nothing for me will ever be the same. The fear that once controlled my every thought is gone. I go into the house and my mother tells me to sit down. When I do, she begins to yell at me about fighting in school. She tells me how none of her kids got in trouble for fighting in school. That is a really weird thing about my family: My mother had four children with another man before she married my father. She considers them to be her children. She considers me to be my father's child. When I argue with my half-sister, my mother will scream for me to leave her daughter alone.

She is only slightly drunk right now, so she's more coherent than her later drunken stages. My mother continues to yell at me. I then go into a world where I can't hear a thing she's saying. My newly discovered anger is taking me again.

I suddenly stand up and yell, "Shut up and leave me alone. I don't need a lecture from my mother the drunk."

My mother takes a deep breath and stands up. In her low angry voice, she says, "What did you say to me, boy?"

I am not aware of what I am doing, but I go over to the stove, grab a clean frying pan, and throw it at her. After it bounces off a wall, I say, "See, you're not the only one who can throw things around here. Just think, I'm not even drunk."

It is the second time today I see fear in someone's eyes. My mother is horrified. She is scared right now. I think about this for a second and it feels really good.

My mother points to the door and screams, "Get out, you rotten good-for-nothing."

She then lets out a series of expletives that would impress a sailor.

I slowly go to the door. I open it, turn back, and say, "Glad we had this talk."

A few hours later, I hear my father standing on the front porch yelling my name.

I go to the house and walk up the steps. My father is upset.

"I heard about your fight today. What do you have to say for yourself?"

I tell my dad what happened. He always encouraged me to get into fights when I was younger and scared. Now, I am not scared. I think he'll be proud of me.

"You can't do stuff like that anymore. That kid's father owns the garage where I take my car. Now, I'll probably have to take my car to another garage that's not close. Do you understand what you've done to me?"

"He started it," I yell.

My father waves his hand to dismiss what I've told him and says, "I don't care, you put me in a bad position with my car."

I can't believe what I'm hearing. When I stand up to a bully and win a fight, it is all about how it inconveniences his car repairs.

I am so angry. My nose and eye are swollen. I have bruises on my arms and my head still hurts. I realize I don't know my father. He feels like a stranger to me.

"In case you care, I'm okay."

"Well, that's good."

"I'm not going to apologize to him, if that's what you want. I'll apologize to the janitor, but not him."

"The janitor?"

I guess the principal left that part out.

"Is there anything else you want to talk about? I want to go back and lay down."

"Yeah, why did you throw a frying pan at your mother?"

"What difference does it make? She throws lots of stuff at me like bottles, ashtrays, and other things."

"I don't care. She's your mother. You shouldn't do stuff like that to her."

"So, because she's my mother she can throw things at me with no problem? Is that what you're saying?"

"Don't you start. You're making my life difficult around here with the way you behave. You need to stop it."

My anger starts to take control of me again and I blurt out, "You're making my life difficult by hiding from everybody in your bedroom all the time."

My father turns away and his hands form into fists. His lips curl and he shakes his head. He is trying to control his anger. Without looking at me, he points down the steps and yells for me to leave. He calls me a few choice words. As I am walking away, he yells, "You're a lot of trouble, do you know that? A lot of trouble."

I turn and watch my father go back into the house. I fight back the urge to start yelling at him. I don't know what's wrong with me. After slowly walking away, I return to my sanctuary in the woods. I feel angry, alone, and have a desire to destroy things. I try to read, but it's too much of a struggle. I then find a big thick branch. I take it and start hitting a tree. I don't know how long I hit the tree but by the time I'm done, I'm sweaty, out of breath, and my hands hurt. I feel much better.

It's the day after school is out for the summer. I've spent the morning going on a bike ride with a kid who goes to another school and doesn't live too far away. In the afternoon, I walk down to the hospital where my father works as a maintenance man. They have college kids who go to some program there in the summer. This year's college kids like to play baseball. They invite me to be part of their nightly games. I anticipate a summer of playing in Little League games, playing baseball in the evenings with these guys, and going on bike rides with my new friend. I'm really happy.

Happiness always has a way of slipping away from me. Life seems to wait until I'm enjoying things before it makes its move.

I am at the hospital playing baseball and it's the evening. After being in a Little League game earlier in the day, I spent time with my new friend exploring a creek near his house. Tonight, I'll listen to our big-league team's game on the radio. I feel great.

I haven't been home all day. I'm having a good game when one of the college kids comes out of the hospital and yells my name. I tell her that's me and everybody stops playing. She tells me she just got a call and I'm to go home immediately. I didn't want to stop playing, but I know this changes everything. The college kids are nice about it and tell me to come back if I can.

I'm furious. What could my parents have done now? They must have screwed up in a big way for someone to call the hospital. I slowly take my bike down a large open field. I ride across the paved road and get to the cinder road that goes to my house. When I get to the top, I see the police cars. I can't help but sigh and think to myself, *this can't be happening again.*

As I get closer to the house, I see my dad being led out in handcuffs. His face is bloody. My father can't stop yelling bad things at my mother. My mother emerges from the house yelling things just as bad to him. Her face is also bloody and one eye is swollen. I just stand there watching the scene unfold. My half-sister notices I'm there. She comes over and puts her arms around me. She's crying and is frantic. I want to have feelings for her. I want to care that she's upset, but I don't. I gently pat her back and push her back.

"What happened?" I ask.

"Mom was drinking as usual. Your father came home and they started arguing. One thing led to another and before I knew it, they were hitting one another. I tried to stop it, but I got pushed out of the way. She hit him in the face with a skillet, and he hit her with his fists. They wouldn't stop. Mom took your father's car keys and wallet and threw them outside. When he went to go get them, she locked all the doors. He put his fist through a window and opened up the door. By that time someone had called the police, and they got here just in time. The police tried to get your father to stop, but he wouldn't, so they arrested him. It was awful," she replies.

I know I should be upset, but the only feeling I have is anger. I should probably be concerned about my parents, but I'm not. I should feel bad for my half-sister, but I don't. I try to think about what would be the best thing to do. After looking inside, the house, I see the entire downstairs is trashed. There is broken glass all over the front carpeting where my dad put his fist through a window. I tell my half-sister when she gets her mother cleaned up and in bed to come and get me in the woods. I'll help her clean things up.

I get my canvas bag from the stone house and set things up in the woods. I have a small transistor radio in there now, so I can still listen to baseball games. I don't understand why I'm not as upset as I should be about what just happened. I'm only worried because I know this will change my life. I don't know how, but it will be forever changed. I try to relax and not think about it. Baseball is the only thing I let into my mind.

CHAPTER 3

A Grand Adventure

One evening, I sleep in the house because it was raining during the night. I've been busy avoiding my mother and half-sister following the police incident. My father isn't permitted to come to the house. I stopped going in and out of the doors of the house. When I want to leave, I simply go out of my bedroom window and onto the roof of the front porch. I then climb down the drainpipe. It's also easy to climb up it.

The people at the hospital like me. The night watchman is a black man they call Smitty. He lets me go on his rounds around the hospital with him. He loves baseball as much as I do. Smitty sometimes treats me to stories of when he played in the Negro leagues until he got too old. I heard about his team traveling to different towns and how he batted against the baseball legend Satchel Paige. Smitty has a gold tooth you can't help but notice when he smiles. He smiles a lot.

The hospital has a huge kitchen. I enjoy walking and talking with Smitty as he does his rounds. He always takes a key from a hidden spot on a wall inside the hospital and goes inside. He has to put a key from different locations in the hospital in this box he carries with him. It records the date and time Smitty has been there. When we're in the hospital, he sometimes gets us ice cream or maybe a bottle of root beer from the kitchen. Smitty shows me how to move things around after you take something so nobody notices.

One evening I'm hungry and don't want to go back to my house. I take the key from the wall in the hospital and let myself into the hospital's kitchen. They have many sandwiches made in the refrigerators. Huge containers with small bags of chips. I take some and have a feast. I continue going back there occasionally to get canned stuff for my canvas bag. One time, they have huge boxes filled with chocolate bars and another time there are several trays of roasted chicken. Being able to get food from the hospital makes it easier for me to stay away from my house for long periods of time. In many ways, I feel I can take care of myself.

On the morning after the rainy night, my mother yells up the steps for me to get dressed and come downstairs. This rarely happens. My mother and half-sister have always been happy to leave me alone. I ask why, and she tells me to just do it.

I go downstairs and there is a white van parked outside of the house. A man with a dark green baseball cap is sitting in the driver's seat smoking a cigarette and looking off into space. My mother and half-sister have on nice clothes. I'm told to go and get in the van. I ask why and my mother tells me to just do it. I stand my ground and ask again why I have to get in the van. My half-sister tells me this isn't the time to talk about it. I know it's going to be another rainy day. I will probably have to spend it in my house or the stone house. I figure since I can't play baseball today, I might as well get in the van.

I realize we're going to the city and it will be a long drive. My mother and half-sister are whispering to one another during the trip. The van stops at the Greyhound bus station. I watch as a large trunk is taken out of the back of the van. My half-sister tells me to take one half, and we carry it into the bus station. We go to baggage check-in and drop off the trunk.

When the woman behind the counter asks the destination, my half-sister says, "Sacramento, California."

I'm instantly terrified. I don't want to go to Sacramento, California. I don't want to go anywhere. I look at my half-sister and say, "I don't want to go there. I want to stay here."

She tells me we have no choice. The hospital owns the farmhouse where we live and because of the fight and the police, they told us we couldn't live there anymore. I can feel tears streaming down my cheeks. I'm instantly told to stop by my mother and to quit embarrassing her in public.

I feel numb as we sit waiting for a bus. I don't want to talk to my mother or half-sister. I want to go back and finish playing in the Little League season. I want to go to the woods. I want to talk to Smitty. I want my orange bike. I want to play baseball with the summer college kids. I feel like a prisoner.

"Maybe I'll just leave and go back on my own," I say to my half-sister.

"How are you going to do that? We're in the middle of the city. You don't know anybody or how to get back there. You can't walk there. Face it, you're going to Sacramento, so just stop making a big deal out of it," she responds.

We eventually get on the bus. My body feels like lead. My mother and half-sister are in seats behind me and I sit in front of them. A man sits next to me and smiles.

The man looks at me and says, "You, okay? You look sort of off."

"I'm okay," I mumble.

I close my eyes and try to sleep. I'm bored and unhappy. I'm worried about Larry the opossum. He's going to be looking for cans to lick clean. I think I may never again hear an owl announce my arrival in the woods. My heart is breaking.

I hear my mother and half-sister talking behind me. My half-sister thinks I'm asleep, so she whispers to my mother and asks why she brought me. My mother says as long as I'm with them, my father will send money. If things don't work out, they can always go back to my father as long as I'm with them. My half-sister doesn't like it, but she understands my mother's reasoning. I then go to sleep wishing I wasn't on a bus heading toward Sacramento, California.

My half-sister tells me we are going to be on the bus for three days. I wake up on the second day and look out of the window to see a new world. The long green pastures I had known my whole life are gone. I see open prairies for the first time in my life. I am amazed at how flat and huge the land is in this place. I see places that have hundreds of cows and guys riding horses like in western movies. We stop at a place to eat dinner. Most people in the restaurant are wearing cowboy hats and have on cowboy boots. I just stare at everyone. This may be one of the best places I've ever seen. I remember a previous trip out west, but I quickly push it out of my mind. I'm forbidden from talking about it.

When it comes time to get on the bus, I get to my seat and a guy wearing a cowboy hat and boots sits next to me. I ask him about his hat and boots. He tells me that where he grew up, this is what everybody wears. The bus ride is long, and I'm treated to stories about cattle roundups, being in rodeos, and living on a cattle ranch. He tells me about branding cattle and getting them to market. Riding horses from early in the morning to late at night. It is like I'm talking to someone right out of a western movie. I think about Nevada but quickly let it go.

He asks me where I'm from and I tell him. He asks what I like to do when I'm not in school, and I tell him about my love of baseball. The man knows nothing about baseball. He's never played it or watched it. I'm speechless. I had no idea somebody could live in this world and know nothing about baseball. I quickly realize he and I are from two very different worlds.

The last guy to sit with me is a person from India. He is the first person I have ever met from another country. The way he pronounces words sounds different to me. I get to hear about his life in India and living in one of the most crowded cities in the world. He tells me about traveling by rickshaw and how different the food is in India. The man from India shows me pictures of his home. I'm fascinated.

The trip is making it possible for me to meet people from different places. I begin to feel happy talking with all of these people and learning about them. I realize I just might be having a grand adventure.

After spending days on a bus, we arrive in Sacramento, California. It's a city with lots of stores and people different from anything I have ever seen. My half-sister took two years of Spanish class in school and points out people speaking Spanish. They're everywhere. I can't understand anything they're saying.

We make our way to a hotel. My half-sister and I carry the trunk upstairs and put it in the room. She and my mother open it up and start pulling out clothes. I then realize it doesn't contain my baseball cards or baseball glove or baseball or hat. Except for some clothes, shoes, socks, jacket, and underclothes, there is nothing else of mine in the trunk. All of my stuff is gone.

I start to get upset when I realize this and tell my half-sister and mother. They both get angry at me. My mother tells me to stop being such a squall baby. I always heard how I cried the most out of all of her children. She always tells me to quit being such a squall baby when I cry. My half-sister tells me my father will probably keep my stuff and I can get it later. This makes me feel a little calmer.

The time spent in the hotel is only a few days. My mother leaves in the mornings with my half-sister to look for work. I'm left alone in the hotel room and told to watch television and occupy myself. I am not to leave the hotel room under any circumstances.

On the second day, I am bored with television. I start walking around and looking outside the window. Watching the people going in and out of stores and walking along the sidewalks I wonder about their lives. I want to know how many of them like baseball and if they play it or watch games. I want to believe some of them love baseball like me.

I suddenly decide that I've had enough. I leave the room and go down the stairs to the lobby. Yesterday, I noticed there were baseball magazines on some of the tables. I get a few and make my way to one of the hotel's chairs and start reading. The lobby is empty except for me and the guy behind the hotel's desk.

I notice a guy come from behind who then sits down in a chair right beside me. I look at him. He's a thin man who needs a shave. The aroma of cigarettes and whiskey coming from him is almost unbearable.

He looks at me and says, "How you doing, kid?"

"Okay," I respond.

The guy looks around then looks at me and says, "Hey, you ever kissed a man? I mean really kissed him with your mouth open and tongues touching?"

I'm starting to get angry.

I say, "No, why don't you go away? I don't like you."

I roll up the magazine and I'm ready to hit him. He then grabs my legs and whispers into my ears, "I've got money. I can be good to you if you're good to me. Know what I mean?"

My anger takes control. I stand up and start hitting the guy in the face with a rolled-up magazine. I start calling him every curse word I have in my vocabulary. He then stands up, starts swearing, and grabs me. I kick him in the groin. He hits me but I don't feel it. I hit him in the face. The two of us are going at it when I see someone grab him from behind and then someone grabs me.

The man from behind the desk is there and yells, "What the hell is going on?

The guy points to me and yells, "I was minding my own business when this young punk attacked me for no reason. I think he wants my money. He needs to be arrested."

Now I'm really angry and yell, "Out of all the chairs in this lobby this asshole sits down next to me and asks if I've ever kissed a man and talks about money if I'm good to him. He grabbed my leg, and so I hit him in the face with a magazine."

I'm told to calm down. The man from the desk asks me if I have a room in the hotel. I say yes and show him the key from my pocket. The other guy confesses he doesn't have a room in the hotel. He's told there is no reason for him to be in the hotel and he must leave immediately. The guy says he's going to get the police and come back and have me arrested for assault. Somebody yells he'll be arrested for trespassing.

As the guy leaves the hotel, I'm looking for something to hit him. A baseball bat, a stick, but I don't see anything. I want to chase after him and hit him. I want to go after him and hurt him. I feel rage on levels I never experienced before in my life.

I look at the man from the desk and apologize for ruining the magazine. He tells me not to worry about it and says I can take any of the baseball magazines on the tables that I want. He tells me I should then go back to my room and read them. I can't believe my luck. There are four of the latest baseball magazines on these tables. There would have been a fifth one but it got destroyed when I rolled it up and beat the guy in the face with it.

When my mother and sister come back to the hotel room later, they ask me where I got the baseball magazines. I tell them what happened, and they don't believe me. My half-sister says I must have stolen them. I get angry and call her a liar. I yell that she doesn't know what she is talking about. My mother says she doesn't care if I stole them and to be quiet and leave her daughter alone.

One more time in my life I've told the truth and people created a lie to ignore it. I start to believe people don't want to hear the truth. They want to hear a lie that fits into their perception of things. If the truth isn't something they like, they'll just hold on to a lie they like better.

The next day as we're leaving the hotel, I have the baseball magazines. I ask my mother and half-sister to meet the guy behind the desk. I hand him the baseball magazines. He tells me to keep them. He apologizes to my mother about what happened the day before with the leg-grabbing guy. I'm smiling and feeling happy as we walk out of the hotel.

I go beside my mother and say, "See, I told you what happened and you didn't believe me."

My mother stops in the middle of the sidewalk. She points her index finger at me and says, "Look, you little shit. I never said it didn't happen. I said I didn't know. Now, just stop it. You're too much like your father, you know that?"

My half-sister gets between me and my mother. She gets close to my face and says, "You always do this. You make a big deal about nothing. So what? A guy grabbed your leg and you hit him with a magazine. So, what's the big deal?"

They both look at me like they're disgusted and continue walking down the sidewalk.

There it is again. They changed the truth. My mother and half-sister are liars. They accused me of stealing the baseball magazine when I didn't. Now, they're acting like they never accused me of anything. They know that's not the truth. I begin to realize when liars are confronted with the truth, it will make their lies worthless. They just as quickly change things and believe a new lie to be their truth.

My mother and half-sister are in front of me as we go down the city sidewalk. I am walking behind them thinking to myself that I now know what it feels like to hate people. I just wonder if I will control it or if it will control me. Right now, I don't care.

CHAPTER 4

A New World

The temperature outside today is really high. My half-sister and I are carrying the luggage trunk through a door between two stores. We go up a long flight of stairs. My mother takes out a key and opens one of the many doors. When we go inside, there is an old wooden table with four chairs. The bedroom has a large bed and dresser. The living room has a couch and chair as well as a black and white television. There is a small kitchen and bathroom off to the side. This is our new home, and I hate it.

I miss my bedroom and my stuff from the old farmhouse. I miss the woods. I miss so many things. I have nobody who will listen to me. I feel very alone.

My mother and half-sister sleep in the big bed in the bedroom. I get to sleep on the couch. It creeks and has a bad smell. The black and white television only has a few stations that work. I'm able to watch some professional baseball games between teams on the west coast. I can usually only watch baseball games until my half-sister and mother take over the television.

I don't know where my mother and half-sister go during the day. When they're gone, I'm told to never leave the apartment. I try to stay in the apartment and just watch television. I try to occupy myself with reading baseball magazines, but I can't. The day is just too nice.

I wonder how my Little League team is doing this year. I think about playing baseball with the college kids at the hospital. I hate being in this small, smelly apartment. I decide to go out for a walk.

The front door to the apartment goes onto a city street. The back door goes into a small yard. On the other side are sidewalks, rows of houses close together, and apartment buildings. I start walking and I'm enjoying the day.

I see what appears to be a baseball field in the distance. I slowly walk up to it. There are kids my age playing baseball. I stand at the fence and watch them. They're all speaking Spanish. Their home plate is a sandbag, the other bases are hubcaps from cars. They're good. The kid who is pitching is very good. They're so involved in their game; they don't immediately notice me.

The pitcher is a tall kid wearing a dark baseball cap, white muscle shirt, and blue jeans. He looks up and notices me. His face becomes angry. He throws down his baseball glove and walks off the baseball field, comes up to me, and pushes me in the chest. He says something in Spanish.

"I don't understand Spanish," I yell.

The pitcher just pushes me again and says, "Oh yeah? Why you watching us play baseball, gringo kid? Huh? Why don't you go back to your neighborhood? This is where Mexican kids play baseball, whether you like it or not. You know that, gringo kid?"

He pushes me one last time and I yell, "Wait, wait, wait just a minute. I'm not from around here. I'm really a long way from my home. I love playing baseball. I haven't been able to play baseball for a long time. I just liked watching you play because I miss playing it. I'm sorry. I'll go now. I won't come back. I won't bother you again. I just miss playing baseball is all. I'm sorry I made you mad."

The pitcher's face is no longer angry. I turn and start walking away. He and the other kids start speaking Spanish. I wipe the tears from my eyes. I want to run and not stop until I'm dead.

I don't get too far until I feel something pull my shirt. I look over and it's one of the kids who had been playing baseball.

He looks at me and seems upset. The kid says, "Play baseball, come, play baseball."

I turn back and the pitcher is motioning for me to come back.

I walk back and he says, "Yeah, you don't look like you're from around here. Okay, you want to play baseball. You any good?"

"I do well in Little League."

"Little League? What in the hell is Little League? We don't got nothing like that around here. Come on, I'll pitch to you for a while."

I've never known anybody who didn't know about Little League. This is a different world.

They only have one baseball bat and it is covered in black electrical tape. This is done when a wooden bat is cracked. This one has been cracked more than once.

The first pitch goes right at my head. I move away at the last second and avoid getting hit. The kids in the outfield laugh.

"Hey gringo kid, how you like playing Mexican-style baseball?"

Now I'm angry. He wants to humiliate me in front of his friends. My little league coach taught me how to surprise someone who is trying to purposely hit you with a pitch. You wait until they're about to release the ball, take a step back and then try your best to hit the ball.

The pitcher again throws the ball right at me. I quickly take a step back and swing the bat. I connect and the ball goes sailing. I run to first, then second. I have no third base coach to tell me what to do, so I run for home. The catcher is trying to block the plate. I do a foot slide between his legs and touch home before he gets the ball. I stand up and start dusting myself off.

The pitcher walks over to me. He's speaking Spanish with the other kids then turns to me and says, "You hit pretty darn good there, gringo kid."

I smile and say, "Thanks."

He holds out his hand and says, "My name is Javier."

I shake his hand and tell him my name. Javier is two years older than me. I'm introduced to the other kids in the group. They're named Pablo, Carlos, Jose, Diego, Alberto, and Enrique. The kids are my age except for Carlos who is a year younger. Javier apologizes for being so tough on me earlier. He tells me they've got to be willing to fight to protect their area. If not, kids from other neighborhoods will come and take over their ball field. Then they won't have any place to play baseball. I begin to realize how much they live in a world I know nothing about.

Enrique asks me what I'm doing here. I again feel the shame and embarrassment as I have so many times before. They don't want to know the truth. I decide it's best to tell them a lie and say we're visiting relatives. When I tell them about the apartment building where I'm staying, Carlos asks if my mother is a whore. He says only whores and drug addicts live in those apartments. I don't know what to say. I don't have a baseball glove so Enrique quickly goes to his house and gets his older brother's glove. He says his older brother is away in the Army.

We play baseball until it is almost dark. They tell me to meet them around the same time tomorrow at the baseball field. I go back to the apartment by crossing a yard and go up the back way. I left the back door unlocked, but it is locked now. I look in the window and see my mother and half-sister sitting at the kitchen table. I notice my mother is drinking. I hate how I have to go inside and deal with them. I have no woods, no canvas bag, and no money. I knock on the door and my half-sister eventually lets me in. After getting yelled at for leaving the apartment, I get lectured by my mother about always making things so difficult for her. My half-sister joins in and won't let it go. I feel trapped, but I'm determined to figure something out tomorrow to avoid coming back here.

During the next few days, I play baseball with Javier and his friends. These kids rule their neighborhood. They know everybody and everyone knows them. When I'm walking with them, I often get strange looks from people. I'll hear them say things in Spanish as I go past. It doesn't bother me; I have no idea what they're saying.

It is raining one day, and the baseball field is very muddy. Javier tells me they lost a baseball in someone's backyard. They ask me to go get it and I agree. I walk into the backyard and can't find the baseball. I then see the dog. It starts to run after me and when

I get near the gate, Javier and the others close it. I quickly climb a fence and try to get over it. On the other side is a dog barking just as much. I'm trapped. Javier and the other guys are laughing at the sight of me clinging for life on a fence.

I get to the top and reach up to grab a tree branch hanging over the fence. I stand up. The tree branch isn't strong enough for me to get on it, but I can hold on to it and balance. I keep moving back and forth to avoid falling. Javier and the other kids are laughing and speaking Spanish.

I hear one of them say, "Keep going and give us a good dance gringo kid, and then we'll open the gate."

Those guys have a good laugh at that one. I'm trying to slowly move my way down the down fence toward a gate on the other side of the backyard. I'm really scared. Then I see a woman come out of the house. She whistles and claps her hands. The dog goes to her, and she puts it inside the house.

She looks at me and says, "You down. Down here now."

I climb down from the fence. She looks at me and says, "Javier?"

I say, "Yes."

She seems angry and motions for me to follow her.

The woman leads me into her house and motions for me to sit at her kitchen table. I figure I'm in trouble. Everything is really clean in the house. There are statues and pictures of the Virgin Mary all over. This woman goes out of the front door and yells for Javier. He comes to her, and they have a discussion in Spanish. Javier is looking down when the woman hits him in the head and points to me. Javier comes into the house and sits down at the kitchen table across from me. The woman gives us each a plate with a burrito on it. I'd never had one before, but it tastes so good to me.

Javier says, "Sorry if we messed you up a bit. This is my aunt's house. Her dog would never harm you. He just barks because he wants to play. I know he's scary, but he wouldn't hurt you."

"I guess it was funny. I didn't know what I was going to do."

Javier laughs and says he loved my balancing act. Jose is calling it the gringo kid dance. Javier's aunt comes over and says something to him in Spanish.

"My aunt wants to know what you're doing in our neighborhood."

I repeated the lie about visiting relatives. His aunt wants to know where my relatives live. I say I don't know, but my mother goes to see them every day. Javier and his aunt look at one another. Like with so many people in the past, I know they don't believe me. Javier and his aunt speak a bit more in Spanish. I am glad I can't understand what they're saying. I would probably be embarrassed. Javier and his aunt know there is something wrong with me and my family. They're just too polite to talk about it in English.

Javier and the other kids in the neighborhood are good at playing baseball, but they are even better at stealing things. They teach me how to take stuff from stores. Candy, baseball cards, and a hat were all fruits of our petty larcenies. They never get caught. Once, Carlos stole some cigars. We all decided we would try to smoke them. All of us got dizzy and threw up except for Javier. Enrique said that is because Javier was born in a tobacco field in Fresno, California. Javier corrected him and said it was a strawberry field.

Some of the kids would be gone for days to go work in the fields with their parents. I've been with these guys every day for a few weeks, and I'm enjoying it a lot. One day Javier tells me it is time I meet Juan. I have no idea what this means.

Javier, Pedro, and I walk a long way to some kind of industrial area. Sitting in a nice car is a very well-dressed man. This is Juan. Javier and Pedro speak in Spanish to him. Suddenly, they step away and motion for me to come up to the car.

Juan takes off his sunglasses and smiles. He has dark hair, brown eyes, and a thin mustache. Juan looks at me and says, "A white kid. I love it. I can use you. You like to make money?"

His accent is thick but I understand him.

"Yeah, I wish I had some."

"Well don't worry about it. I know how you can make sixty dollars. You want to make sixty dollars?"

"Yeah, what do I have to do?"

Juan reaches over to the driver's side of the car and hands me a package.

"Just deliver this to the address on the front and hand it to Roberto Martinez. Don't let anyone else touch the box. You only hand it to Roberto Martinez. You will know him by a rooster he has tattooed on his hand. Can you do this?"

"Sure, that's it?"

"That's it. He's going to give you some money in an envelope. You bring it back here tomorrow and give it to me. I'll give you sixty dollars."

"What's in the box?"

Before the words are out of my mouth, Javier is in my face. He's saying, "Don't ever ask that question. You never, ever ask that question. You don't need to know what's in the box. Just deliver it like Juan told you."

I look at Juan. He puts on his sunglasses and says, "Because you're white, not from around here, and don't know much, I'll forgive your question. You ask questions like that again, and I won't be your friend. I'm sure you don't want me to be your enemy."

"No, I don't."

Juan claps his hands and says, "Good, tomorrow come here with the envelope containing the money, and we'll be friends."

The driver-side window is rolled up and Juan's car starts going toward the road.

We go back to the house of Javier's aunt. He gets a brown bag and puts Juan's package in it. Javier walks with me down to a busy city street. It's a long walk. There is an old building with a sign on the front about it being an office building. Javier tells me where to go and deliver the package. I ask him why he isn't doing this.

Javier says, "Too many Mexican kids going into a place carrying bags will draw too much attention. Nobody will suspect you. It's okay because Juan lets me get money in other ways."

I go to the building and walk up to the door as Javier told me. I knock on the door. A woman opens it up and says, "What do you want?"

I tell her I'm there to deliver a package to Robert Martinez.

She holds out her hand and says, "You can just give me the package."

"No, I can only give this to Robert Martinez," I say.

She turns and walks away from the door. After she yells something in Spanish, a guy comes out of an office. It's him, the guy with the rooster tattoo on his hand. He motions for me to follow him.

We go back to a nicely decorated office. Robert Martinez sits down at a desk and I hand him the bag with the package inside. He takes it out, opens it a bit, and looks inside for a few seconds.

The man then opens up a desk drawer and takes out an envelope. He tosses it on the desk and says, "Here you go. So, Juan is using a white kid now. He is very smart. You take this back to Juan. What's your name?"

"My name is Mark."

The man takes out some money from his pocket. It is two twenty-dollar bills, and he hands them to me.

"This is your commission. Don't tell Juan about this, it will be our little secret."

I put the envelope in one pocket and the two twenty-dollar bills in another pocket.

"Is that it?"

"Unless you got another package, that's it."

I turn around and leave. The office door hasn't been closed. I walk out and close it. It's a long walk back to the neighborhood. I see Javier. He asks how things went, and I tell him it was so easy.

I'm worried about the envelope. I just want to get it to Juan. I feel a little scared.

The next day I go to the spot where I'm supposed to meet Juan. Javier is there waiting for me. He seems nervous for some reason. Juan's car pulls up. The driver's window comes down and Juan is there smiling at me.

"So, my gringo friend, how was your first day on the job?"

I hand Juan the envelope. He opens it up and begins counting the money inside.

"You know, he gave me forty dollars and said it was my commission. I know you agreed to give me sixty dollars. Do you want to just give me twenty dollars? I mean, I really appreciate you letting me have this money."

I pull out the forty dollars and show him. Javier seems very relieved. Juan starts laughing.

"Only a white boy from another part of the country would be this honest. I've had little assholes take money from the envelope and not tell me about the commission money. You passed, kid. You're my friend."

Juan and Javier talk in Spanish for a while. Juan hands me a twenty-dollar bill. He turns on his car's radio. A station playing Spanish music is turned up loud. The driver's side window goes up, and his car starts going toward the road.

Javier and I start walking toward the baseball field.

I say, "What did he mean I passed and I'm his friend? I don't get it."

"You don't know what just happened, do you?"

"I guess I don't."

"Juan wants people working for him he can trust to tell him everything. This was a test to see if you would not steal from the envelope, come clean about the commission money, and tell him everything."

"What would have happened if I kept the money?"

"I'm glad you didn't. Juan told me if you kept it, I was to take it from you and give it to him. He'd never have anything to do with you again."

I still didn't understand what just happened. This is not how I envisioned my first job. I spend the rest of the day doing what I do when the world confuses me—I play baseball.

During the next few weeks, I become part of the local Mexican kids' group. I am invited to a sleepover at Pablo's house with the other kids. I am invited to Diego's birthday party with everybody and have my first experience with a pinata. I spend days watching television with the others at Enrique's home. They work at teaching me some Spanish. It's not long before I can say most of the Spanish swear words. Javier says I need to know them not to swear at any Mexicans, but to know when they're swearing at me. I keep repeating the same lies about my mother and family. I don't want them to know anything. I fear it could ruin things between us. The kids and adults eventually stop asking.

My last job for Juan consists of getting a bicycle. I am told someone has stolen it from him. I go onto a porch at dusk and take the bike. It's obviously a new bike. I ride like the wind as I was told by Juan. A guy in his twenties starts chasing me. I feel good understanding all the Spanish swear words he is calling me. I'm not used to riding bikes around cars, but I do pretty well. I get away from him and make it to the area near a manufacturing plant like Juan told me. There is a pickup truck there. When I arrive, I quickly get off the bike. Juan and Javier put the bike in the back of the truck. I don't understand what they're saying to each other, but the man drives away. Juan gives me and Javier twenty dollars.

As we're walking away, I look at Javier and say, "Why did Juan put his bike in that guy's truck?"

Javier starts laughing.

"You don't get anything, do you? That wasn't Juan's bike, he just told you a story. The guy in the truck is one of Juan's bosses. He wanted the bike for his kid and Juan got it for him."

"You mean we stole it?"

"What do you think? Sometimes you're so stupid. That's how we do things around here, if you haven't noticed. Be glad you got twenty dollars"

A few days later, I make it back to the apartment when it's dark outside. My mother is pretty drunk and won't look at me. My half-sister also seems pretty upset about something.

I say, "What's wrong?"

"It's your father. Mom can't find a job, and he says he's not going to send any more money unless you live with him. We're going back," says my half-sister.

My mother opens a new can of beer and says, "My whole life, men have done nothing but make me miserable. I hate you all."

"I don't want to go back. Me, Javier, and the rest of the kids are playing a baseball game against kids from another neighborhood tomorrow. They need me. This can't be happening. I have to stay here," I yell.

My half-sister says, "What are you going to do? Think the family of one of your Mexican friends will take you in? We're leaving tomorrow and you're coming with us. You don't have a choice. Blame your father if you want to blame someone."

It is happening to me again. I started to be happy. I'm getting good at swearing in Spanish during baseball games. The other kids like me. Their families like me. They're my friends. I have no friends back there. I go outside and sit down on the steps up to the apartment. I let the tears pour down my cheeks. If my mother sees me crying, she'll be furious. I have that heavy feeling in the center of my chest again.

The next day I feel really sad. I'm struggling with my half-sister to take the trunk down the steps. We put it on the sidewalk and wait for a cab. I see Javier and the rest of the kids. When they see me, they quickly come over.

My mother is a little drunk and looks awful. My half-sister has been giving me a hard time since I woke up today. I'm having those feelings of embarrassment and shame as the kids walk toward us.

"What's going on? We have a big game to play today," says Javier.

"Not me, I'm going back. We're leaving. I'm sorry," I respond.

Javier speaks in Spanish to the other kids, and they seem upset. There is an uncomfortable silence.

Javier says, "That's sad, amigo. I want you to know, I'm gonna miss you. You're the first white kid I ever got to know."

The other kids say how they're also going to miss me. I have that heavy feeling in my chest again. I'm fighting the tears. Javier then asks my half-sister if she has a pen and paper. I'm surprised when she opens her purse and hands them to him. She then tells me to hurry up. Javier writes on the paper and hands it to me. He gives the pen and paper back to my half-sister.

"What's this?" I ask.

Javier says, "This is my address, you write to me, okay?"

I take the paper and put it in my pocket.

"I will write to you."

Javier then does something I never experienced before from another kid. He hugs me quickly and pats me on the back.

"You take care and don't forget about us."

The taxi cab pulls up, and the taxi driver gets out and opens the trunk. My sister tells me to put our trunk in the back of the taxi. I swear at her in Spanish.

"What did you just say to me?" asks my half-sister.

I tell her, "I said you're beautiful"

Javier and the other kids laugh. They wave to me as they start walking down the street. It will be the last time I ever see any of them.

CHAPTER 5

A Sad Return

It's the late 1950s and there are two people on an American military base in West Germany. One of them is named Jake and the other is named Amy. Jake has been in the military for over twenty years. He is guaranteed to have a pension for the rest of his life when he gets out. He's not known for his mental abilities, but he is dependable, follows orders well, and people like him. Amy has just gotten divorced for the second time. She has four children from her second marriage. Jake and Amy have three things in common: They both like to drink, smoke, and spend time at the non-commissioned officer's club.

Jake served in World War II and the Korean conflict. He became an orphan at a young age. During his youth, he spent time with relatives who didn't want him and at orphanages. At the age of 17, he joined the Army. He has never known what it is like to be part of a family. Jake has no idea about family life.

Amy's second husband has recently left her for another woman. He doesn't want anything to do with his four children. His focus is on his new wife. As Amy tries to deal with the rejection of her second husband, she knows Jake is attracted to her. They have a good time at the clubs together. She needs a stable income for herself and her four children. Jake's pension makes him very attractive to her. She doesn't like his Eastern European-sounding last name or how he is easily manipulated by other women. Amy believes she has to sacrifice herself to be with Jake for the sake of her children.

Amy and Jake are each in their late 30s when they get married. The two of them agree to not have any children. Jake was wounded during World War II and was told he is now unable to have children.

The marriage is strained from the beginning. Jake doesn't know how to be a father because he never had one. He doesn't understand why Amy's second husband doesn't spend time with Amy's children. Amy is angry at how Jake seems to only want to watch television in the evenings and not spend any time with her and her children. Soon, Jake moves into his own bedroom never to return to sleep in the same room with his wife. He views his role in the family as simply being a provider of shelter, food, and clothing for Amy and her children. Their arguments are a regular occurrence. They get worse when they drink, and they both drink often.

When they are 42 years old, they both get a shock in their life. Amy announces she is pregnant. She is furious with Jake; she believes he has lied to her about not being able to father children. Jake doubts the child growing in Amy could be his. He tells her if he could father children, there would be many of them on the military base. Amy's activities with other men are well-known. Their arguments continue, followed by periods of ignoring one another.

There is talk of giving the child up for adoption. Jake won't have it. He spent time in an orphanage growing up and would never allow that to happen to any child. Amy looks for ways to illegally terminate the pregnancy, but too many people on the base know her and Jake. They both trade their true feelings for an image of being a typical family with four children and one on the way. The two of them protect their ugly truth with well-spoken lies. They become quite skilled at it. Eventually, they begin to believe their lies and doubt the truth.

There we are once again, me and my half-sister, loading our trunk into the baggage claim area at a bus station. We go and get something to eat. The restaurant has burritos and I get one. I can't stop thinking about my Mexican friends and wondering how they're doing with the baseball game. I suddenly realize I left my new baseball glove at Enrique's house. I knew if I took it or anything else back to the apartment, there would be questions I didn't want to answer. Leaving it at Enrique's house just made things easier. I figured he'll probably keep it or give it to his younger brother. There is an empty steel box near the bottom of the apartment building where we stayed. You wouldn't see it unless you knew it was there. I left my new baseball cards and hat in the steel box. I also had a t-shirt, a poster of San Francisco's Candlestick Park, as well as a few baseballs and some other things in there. I wonder what will happen to the stuff of mine in the steel box. I don't want to think about it. It'll make me feel even sadder.

During the days spent on the bus, I watch the landscape change. Dessert and prairies slowly give way to green grass and open pastures. I see large fields of crops as well as barns, animals in the pastures, grain silos, and more. The bus ride seems to go on forever. Sleeping isn't easy, and I just want this trip to be over.

A woman gets on at one of the stops and sits next to me. We start talking. I listen as she tells me stories about her family, and the grandchildren she has that are around my age. She shows me pictures of her grandchildren and lets me know she is going to spend time with them at her son's home. I don't say much; she does most of the talking. The bus stops and we have a meal break. When the woman comes back to her seat on the bus, she hands me some comic books she has bought for me. I thank her and don't know what to say. This is a very nice woman. I show the comics to my mother, so she doesn't accuse me of stealing them. The woman tells my mother that she hopes it is okay with her. My mother tells the woman she doesn't care but doesn't understand why she bought me anything. She then says if I bother her too much to let her know. The woman tells my mother she thinks I'm a nice boy, and she should be proud of me.

My mother laughs. She tells the woman she doesn't know me and would think differently if she had to be my mother. My half-sister and mother then laugh together. I say some swear words in Spanish. The woman gives me a look of shock. Things are quiet between me and the woman until she gets off at the next stop.

When our bus finally arrives in the city, we are met by the same guy in a white van who took us there the first time. After the trunk is loaded in the van, my mother is in the passenger seat, and I'm sitting next to my half-sister.

"Where are we going?" I ask her.

"I don't know. We can't go back to the farmhouse. Your father said he has a place," she responds.

The driver leans back and tells me where we are headed. I am really upset. It's a dirty little town surrounded by steel mills. I imagine we will have one of those houses that are close together with others. I don't care and just want this journey to be over. I'm anxious to sleep in a bedroom again. I'm hoping all my stuff will be there.

When the van stops, it is on a busy little street surrounded by a few stores and quite a few bars. We go to an old and scratched door between two restaurants. My mother opens the door as my half-sister and I go up the long steps to the top carrying the trunk. I'm horrified.

There is some of our furniture, but that's it. In the bedroom is my dad's bed and television. Everything in his closet and bedroom is in order as if my dad is still in the military. In the dining room is my mother's old bed. She tells my half-sister this is where they will sleep. When I ask about my bedroom, I'm told to go to the kitchen. There is a space between a back door and the kitchen table. My old bed and dresser are there. I have no bedroom of my own, and just a space between the kitchen and back door. I ask where I will change my clothes. I'm told in the bathroom. I tell myself all my things must be someplace.

My dad arrives home and I can hear him coming up the back steps. I've not seen him for a few months, and I'm scared for some reason. I'm sitting on my bed when he opens the back door and sees me. He says, "Hello. How are you doing?"

"Okay, I guess"

"Where's your mother?"

"In the living room."

He walks past me and goes down the hall that leads to the living room. I can hear my parents arguing the minute they lay eyes on one another. I never thought about how great it is to not hear them fighting until now. I struggle with my feelings of missing Sacramento, California. My half-sister comes out and tells me we need to go for a walk. She says we need to get out of here for a while. I'm glad for the chance to be away from the sounds of my parents yelling at one another.

The town is much smaller than Sacramento, but it still has quite a few stores. There is a department store, shoe store, and even a sporting goods store. It has more than one bakery and a few restaurants. There are also quite a few bars. There are bars on the town's main street and side streets. My half-sister is hungry but doesn't have any money. I tell her I'll treat her to dinner. She asks about my money, and I tell her I have enough.

As we sit in the restaurant, she says, "Where did you get the money?"

"I had a job in Sacramento."

"What kind of job?"

"I delivered packages for a guy named Juan and did other stuff for him."

"What other stuff?"

"Just stuff, that's it. It doesn't matter. I can't work for him anymore, being here."

She looks around and then looks back at me and says, "I spent five years at the last school. Now, I'm going to be a senior. I have to go to a new school for my senior year. I can't believe this is happening to me. Your father really messed us up this time."

I don't feel like arguing with her. I never even thought about school. This year I'll be in seventh grade and going to a school I've never been to before. I won't know anybody at the school. I think about how those kids at the school will probably live in houses with their own bedrooms. I don't want anybody who knows me to see this awful apartment. I'm really sad.

When we get back to the apartment, my mother informs us she is going to the bar at the end of the block. My half-sister leaves with her. I knock on my dad's bedroom door. He tells me to come in.

"What do you want?" he asks.

I ask, "What happened to all my stuff?"

"I had to get rid of it. You guys left me holding the bag."

"You got rid of all of it?"

"Everything except for what you see in the apartment. What else was I going to do? I couldn't live in the farmhouse anymore. I needed a cheap place to live and there was too much stuff for this apartment. Yeah, I got rid of all of it. What did you expect me to do with it? Hold onto it while you guys played around out there in California?"

I feel sick inside realizing everything I owned is now gone.

"Okay. That's all I wanted to know."

As I start to go, my father says under his breath how getting married and having a kid was the biggest mistake of his life.

I leave the apartment and go walking around. My orange bike, my electric car set, my baseball cards, my sled and posters of baseball players, and everything else I had is now gone. I wonder what happened to my baseball program that had been signed by a major league player. I've got some clothes in the trunk, some money, and the clothes on my back. My parents are back and fighting as usual. In a bar down the street, my mother is now getting drunk, and my half-sister is hurting because she'll spend her senior year at a new high school. I walk past a gas station and notice a newspaper. I stare at it and laugh. My twelfth birthday has come and gone and nobody even noticed.

CHAPTER 6

Struggles Continue

The four of us settle into a routine in the apartment. My father gets up in the morning and, before going to work, takes a fly swatter and kills the cockroaches crawling on the kitchen counter. I clean them up before my mother can see them. She will start yelling at me about being the reason she is in this crappy apartment. I'm always awake before my father goes to work. I can't sleep with my father in the kitchen right next to my bed fixing his breakfast and making coffee.

My mother's drinking routine has changed. She no longer forces me or my half-sister to sit with her at the kitchen table for hours listening to her drunk rantings. Since we live in a town with so many bars, she simply goes down the apartment's front steps, out the front door, and walks half a block to the nearest bar. She couldn't be happier about the convenience of her access to beer.

I still have to pay a price for her drinking. My mother is still pretty drunk during the early morning hours. She calls the apartment at that time. In her drunken speech, she demands that I come and get her.

One time, I ignore her call. I just pick up the receiver and put it down, disconnecting the call. The next thing I know, the bartender from the bar is knocking on the front door. He says someone has to come to get my mother. She is too drunk to walk home.

I give up after I complain to my father about it. He tells me she's my mother and I should just do it. So, I get dressed, go down to the bar, have my drunk mother hang on me, and walk this way back to the apartment in the early morning hours. This happens on school nights and neither my father nor mother seems to care. I know my half-sister is also awake when my drunk mother goes to bed. I don't think either of us sleeps through the night for a long time. This routine only changes when my mother is feeling sick. But she seems to never be so sick she can't go to the bar.

I discover a playground not far from the apartment. There are other kids there. Some are my age and some are younger. I'm asked to join in playing a game of basketball. I'm having fun and enjoying trying to get the rebounds. I get most of them. After fighting for the basketball during a rebound and getting it, a kid named Sean comes up and hits me in the face. He's smaller than me, and I tell him not to do that again. I warn him the second time he does it. When Sean hits me in the face a third time, I lose my temper. I hit him back so hard he falls back and lands on the ground. Sean stands up holding his eye screaming how he is going to get his older brother Tommy. The other kids tell me Tommy is a big kid who is strong and beats up people all the time. They're frightened of him. I suppose I should be scared, but I'm not. I want to see what this Tommy is like. I want to know if he is as tough as the kids are telling me.

We continue to play basketball. About twenty minutes later, I see Sean coming to the playground with a kid about my size and pointing to me. Tommy has on a baseball cap with a car racing emblem on it. He's got black curly hair sticking out on the sides. I stop playing and hold the basketball as he walks up to me. The other kids are standing around like they're about to see the sporting event of the century.

"You the kid who popped my little brother in the face?" says Tommy.

I shrug my shoulders and say, "Yep, that would be me. He hit me in the face twice, and after the third time, I hit him back twice as hard. Wanted to let him know I didn't appreciate him hitting me in the face when I play basketball."

There is a quiet moment. I look him up and down and Tommy does the same to me. He doesn't look scary to me. Tommy looks at his little brother and when he looks at me, he is smiling.

"Thanks for hitting that annoying little asshole. He does that shit to the other kids around here and threatens to get me if they hit him back. I'm glad you hit my pain in the ass little brother."

Sean yells in a whiny voice, "Tommy, I'm telling Dad."

"Tell him, he's tired of you being an asshole to everybody like the rest of us."

When I first saw Tommy coming toward me, I thought we'd get in a fight. I was focused and ready. Now, I laugh.

"Well, if you have any other annoying little brothers that need me to hit them in the face after they've hit me, I won't have any problems with it."

Now Tommy laughs. He holds out his hand and we shake. Tommy tells me to follow him. So, I give the basketball to one of the other kids at the playground and go with Tommy.

As we walk along the sidewalk in front of all the houses, Tommy tells me about the neighborhood. He points out places to avoid. I find out he is in my grade and I wonder why I haven't seen him in school. Tommy then shows me how to go from the playground, down to a park, across a highway, down to railroad tracks. We cross them and go down again to the banks of a large river. There are trees and small patches of woods. It's not ideal, but now I think I have a place where I can escape from my family.

Tommy advises I not spend too much time at the playground. The kids there are little and the ones who are our age have flunked grades and I don't want to be around them. The fall air is cool. Tommy makes a fire near the riverbank, and we sit around talking until it is almost dark. I learn that he lives in an apartment like me. I live above a restaurant, and Tommy's family lives above a bar. In his family, his father drinks and is crazy. His mother and brothers are afraid of his father's temper. Tommy's family knows the restaurant that I live above very well. His father got kicked out of there for knocking over the cash register when he disagreed with the bill. Tommy and his brothers are always told to just do what his father asks because he is their father. We make the long journey back to the playground and part ways. I hope to see him in school. I completely understand Tommy. I just may have found someone who also understands me.

The winter is long and cold. There are many days when my mother stays home rather than face the cold weather and go to a bar. The bar at the end of the street told her to leave and not come back. I ask my half-sister what happened. She tells me I don't want to know.

My mother is back to drinking at the kitchen table again. If I try to sleep, she'll talk to me when I'm in my bed as if I'm next to her. My bed is almost next to her in the kitchen. My half-sister sits with my mother again until early in the morning. I often go into the living room to sleep.

One night in early spring, I'm lying in my bed asleep. I quickly wake up when I hear someone walking up the back steps. Nobody should be walking up the back steps. I see the glow of a cigarette and a man standing at the back door. All of a sudden, I see someone put their fist through the glass on the back door, reach in, and go to unlock the door. I'm quickly out of my bed, hitting the hand in the broken window. I start screaming to my father that someone is trying to break into the apartment. The man outside starts kicking the door and swearing. The door's lock starts to give way. I'm scared out of my mind screaming for my father. I'm trying to push the door closed as the man pushes on the other side to get it open. He's too strong for me. When he uses his weight to hit the door, I go flying back onto the floor. When the man gets in, I see my father, in his pajamas, go past me and start hitting the man with one of his golf clubs. The man gets his hand on the golf club. He and my father are having a tug of war when I quickly grab a broom and start poking the man in the face with it. When he goes to cover his face, my dad starts hitting him again with the golf club. The man swears and goes out the back door and down the steps.

I'm pretty shaken up. My half-sister is standing in the kitchen in a daze with her hands over her mouth. My dad tells me to get a dustpan. We clean-up all the glass. My dad gets some wood and screws. He screws a piece of wood on the back door where the glass has been broken. During the attack and clean up, my father and I don't talk. It feels like neither one of us wants to acknowledge what just happened. He suddenly announces he's going back to bed because he has to go to work tomorrow. I ask him about calling the police. My father tells me they won't do anything as he closes his bedroom door.

As I start to calm down, I get a phone call from my mother at the bar. I've got to get her. My half-sister finally starts to move and goes back to bed. I get my mother and guide her toward her bedroom. She slowly staggers in and I can hear her talking with my half-sister. I'm exhausted and go back to sleep until it's time to get up for school in a few hours.

The next day, I forget about what happened until I get back to the apartment and see the damaged back door. My mother wants to know what happened. I tell her the story, and she thinks I'm lying. My father gets home and she asks him about it. He tells her the same story I had told her. She's convinced my father and I are liars. Later I talk with my half-sister about it.

"Did Mom ask you what happened last night?" I ask.

"She asked me what happened to the back door," she replies.

"Did you tell her about the guy trying to break in?"

"I told her I didn't see it."

"You were standing right there with your hands over your mouth. I saw you."

"I said I didn't see it," she yells.

"You're a liar. You were right there. I saw you," I yell.

"I didn't see it. No wonder mom doesn't want you around. You do nothing but cause trouble. I said I didn't see it."

After that, my half-sister turns and walks away.

One more time somebody in my family embraces a lie because the truth won't give them what they want. My mother would never believe a story about me and my father fighting with an intruder. It is simpler for my half-sister to say she didn't see what happened. It is not easy to tell my mother something she refuses to believe, even if it's the truth. My half-sister has made it possible for my mother's imagination to explain the breaking of the backdoor and the window. I realize she's just trying to survive our situation.

The owner of the building replaces the back door. The new one is much stronger and has better locks. I still struggle to sleep. I put items at the base of the staircase that leads to the back door. If they're moved, they'll make a lot of noise. I buy a baseball bat and keep it under my bed with a large kitchen knife I bought at a local store. If that guy comes back, I want to be ready.

In the spring, my half-sister will graduate from high school. I don't know how I will handle my mother without her. I don't know what will happen, and I'm not looking forward to it. I sense my life could soon be getting even worse.

CHAPTER 7

Half-Sister Army

I am in sixth grade the school year before we had to leave the farmhouse. It's a difficult time for me. I don't do well in school. I'm constantly tired and always feeling stressed about what awaits me when I go home. The other kids ignore me, I'm last at being picked for teams when we play games, and I don't feel any connection to what's happening around me.

There are two sixth-grade classes. A teacher tells the kids of both of the sixth grades they can sign up to learn to play chess during lunch. I'm just like most of the other kids in sixth grade and sign up to learn to play the game of chess. I'm one of the fastest learners. I'm winning games and carefully studying other kids when they win games. Learning the strategy of the game comes easily to me. I soon grasp how you need to think two and three moves ahead. I've had to anticipate the behavior of my parents for years to prepare for what may happen.

After most of the school year is over, the teacher organizes a sixth-grade chess tournament. I easily win my first two games in the tournament. I need to win the next two games to play the winner from the other sixth-grade class. One teacher accuses me of figuring out a way to cheat, and other kids repeat what she is saying. I'm not considered an intelligent kid. Nobody gives me credit except for the teacher who taught me and the other kids to play chess. He tells me being a winner requires dealing with bad losers. The teacher tells the kids and other teachers that cheating is impossible.

It is a struggle, but I win the next two games. The last kid I beat is furious. The teacher calms him down as he yells how he hates me and this game. I just watch and smile at the behavior of the guy who has never gotten anything but the highest scores in school since he started. It feels good.

My picture and the picture of the girl from the other sixth-grade class are put on the bulletin board for those entering the school. Somebody draws on my picture, but I don't care. I still feel good.

On the day of the chess championship game, the teacher announces our names to all the students and parents in the common area where a chessboard is set. The girl and I then begin playing our championship game. It takes a long time. She is good, really good. We go back and forth until we reach a stalemate. There is no way either of us can win the game. The teacher says we are both chess champions. A little certificate is given to each of us with our names on them. I am still accused of cheating by some of the kids in my sixth-grade class.

I take the certificate home and show it to my mother. She and my half-sister cannot believe it. They instantly make jokes about me making the certificate myself, or I paid the girl to play to a stalemate. My mother tells me her kids could have done something like this if they had all of my advantages. She tells me I have everything. I show the certificate to my father and he smiles.

He then rustles my hair and says, "You're an okay kid. That's my boy."

I can't remember the last time I had my father say something so nice to me. I feel so much pride when my father takes the certificate and puts it in his pocket. I'm told he'll give it back to me later; he wants to show some people and then leaves.

My mother has been drinking when my father returns from his club early. He has a package in hand. He says it's for his son, the chess champion. My mother starts yelling about how he never gets anything for my half-sister. She screams how he is a horrible husband and only cares about him and his son. My mother yells how she is sick and tired of putting up with me and my father every day. She continues to scream.

It is a rainy day. My father goes out onto the front porch and throws the package. It hit a tree and chess pieces go everywhere. He then gets in his car and leaves.

I go out into the rain and get the chessboard and chess pieces. I am happy that nothing is broken. The box that holds the chessboard and pieces does have a crack. It is still a nice chess set.

The next day, I try to thank my father for the chess set. He ignores me. I see my certificate sticking out of his coat pocket. It is crumbled up and has been rained on. I take it and put it in my bedroom. I am proud of it, but part of me wishes I hadn't done this since it caused so much trouble.

As I struggle to get through each day in the crappy apartment, I feel bad for my half-sister. She's an attractive girl and the men at the bars where my mother goes to drink aren't always the most respectful to her. She has made a few friends during her senior year and one good one. My half-sister does better in school than I do, and my mother informs me her kids are smarter than me and my father's family.

There comes a time when my half-sister gets a boyfriend. I can't believe it when she asks him to come to our crappy apartment. Why would she want someone to meet our mother or see my father in his bedroom, or even be in this horrible apartment? I don't understand why she would do such a thing. She explains how she feels it will be okay and not to worry.

I come home late one night and get my mother at the bar after her early morning call. I wake up the next day to see my half-sister sitting in the living room with a blank stare. I ask her what's wrong, and she won't talk. She just sits there staring out of the front window. I tell my mother about this, and she says for me to leave her daughter alone.

It appears it only took one visit to our crappy apartment, and one experience with my mother's drinking, to discourage my half-sister's boyfriend. It lasted a few weeks, but it is over now. I can hear my mother telling my half-sister how her boyfriend thought he was too good for us. My mother yells how if that punk doesn't like us then my half-sister doesn't need him.

I am never told what happened. I never know what my mother said to my half-sister's boyfriend. All I know for certain is that things change between my half-sister and my mother after that time. My half-sister starts spending many nights sleeping over at her friend's house. When I see her, she never talks to me. If I try to start a conversation, she always changes the subject. She starts staying away from the apartment just as much as I do.

My half-sister completes twelfth grade. She does not have the highest grades in her class, but she has done well. My mother and father try to talk about what my half-sister wants to do after she graduates from high school. This starts a major argument between my parents. My mother demands that she goes to college. My father says he isn't going to pay for it, and my half-sister's father should pay for it. My mother starts screaming how my father and I are horrible and how I get everything and her daughter gets nothing. The argument lasts for a long time. After they get done throwing things at one another, each goes into their bedroom and slams their doors loudly.

It's late and I'm sitting with my half-sister in the living room. We're watching television with the volume turned low. The last thing either one of us wants is to wake our mother who has been drinking earlier.

"Have you decided what you're going to do after graduation?" I ask.

My half-sister doesn't look at me but says, "Don't worry about it. I'll take care of it."

"What are you going to do?"

"Drop it," she screams.

I'm planning to play pony league baseball this summer. I buy myself a new glove and have enough to pay for the registration and uniform. My dad agrees to sign the papers for me to play. I can now walk to the practice field and the coach tells me someone can take me to and from the away games. I haven't played organized baseball for over a year, and I'm anxious to play in a league again.

Tommy and I are spending more time together. We explore the banks of the river, sit around fires at night, and avoid the messed-up people who occasionally find their way to the river. We make plans to journey to a sunken barge as well as go on bike trips in the summer. He wants to show me a haunted house that has secret rooms in it. I think it will be fun.

We're walking through a parking lot when Tommy notices his friend named Roger in a car. Roger has long bushy brown hair and is wearing a blue jean jacket. We go up to the car and Roger tells us to get inside. We do this; Tommy is in the front passenger seat and I'm sitting in the back and Roger is sitting in the driver's seat. It appears that Roger has noticed this car hasn't been moved from this parking spot for weeks. The door was left open so Roger decided to get inside of it. He is trying to use wires under the steering column to start the car. Tommy tells Roger to give it up, he doesn't know what he's doing. I ask why he wants to do this.

When I say my last word, the car starts up.

Roger sits up in the driver's seat and says, "What do you think about that, assholes?"

Tommy is 13. I will be 13 in the summer and Roger is 14 years old. None of us have any driving experience.

"Let's see what this baby can do," says Roger.

"Have you ever driven a car before?" says Tommy.

Roger laughs and says, "I've watched my dad do it a thousand times. It's not hard."

We start talking about all the great places we can go as the car is carefully backed out of the parking spot by Roger. He then puts it in gear, and we're moving forward. The car goes faster and then faster.

"Slow down," yells Tommy.

Roger screams, "I can't, I don't have my foot on the gas and the breaks aren't working."

All three of us are screaming. When we get to the end of the parking lot, Roger makes a sharp turn to the left to avoid hitting a cement wall. The car goes up on two wheels. Tommy starts calling out to Jesus, and Roger screams he can only talk to God since he's Jewish. The car comes down hard and then goes back and forth before the engine dies. All three of us are tossed around until the car gets stable. Roger holds onto the steering wheel and makes the car coast into a parking spot. We all get out and start running. We're so scared we run past where we live and don't stop until we get to a park in another town.

We sit there panting and nobody is saying anything. Roger then starts laughing.

"We were up on two wheels going down the parking lot. Oh man, that is some shit," says Roger.

"You could've gotten us all killed," Tommy yells.

"But he didn't, and I think it is something. I bet no other kids in this town have done anything like this," I say.

"You should have seen your face," Roger says to Tommy.

I look at Tommy and Roger and say, "You should smell my pants,"

All three of us start laughing.

I'm starting to make some friends. I'm not too close with any of them. I don't know if my parents will do something to cause us to leave this town. I don't want to take a chance of feeling that heaviness in the middle of my chest again.

When I get home, my mother is not at the bar but is drinking at the kitchen table. My half-sister is with her. I walk into the kitchen and neither one of them will look at me or respond to my questions. I begin to walk down the hall.

My mother yells, "Do you know what your father has done to me and my daughter?"

I turn around and say, "What now?"

My mother motions for my half-sister to speak.

My half-sister says, "I've joined the Army. I leave for basic training in two weeks."

I don't know what to say. The next few days my mother treats me as if I don't exist, except for when I have to bring her home from the bars in the early morning hours. My father ignores the entire situation. He just comes home, eats, goes into his bedroom, closes the door, and turns on his television. I spend a lot of time by myself exploring the river. I have no idea how I'll handle my drunk mother without my half-sister. For the first time since we came back, I think about trying to go back to Sacramento.

CHAPTER 8

Affairs of the Inebriated

I write to Javier in Sacramento, and he writes back a few times. They lost the baseball game I couldn't play in on the day I left. Javier tells me in his letter it was close, and he believes they would have won if I had been there. I don't know if he knows how much I wanted to be there with them.

In another letter, I read how Pablo broke his arm climbing a tree, Enrique's family got a dog, and Alberto's mother had a baby girl. In one of my letters, I ask about Juan. Javier doesn't say anything about him in his next letter. We exchange about three letters and the last one I send is returned. On the envelope is a red ink stamp saying the recipient was no longer at that address. When I see the letter, I'm very sad. I wonder what happened to Javier and his family. This turn of events makes me feel even more alone in the world.

My half-sister is going to leave for the Army soon, and my parents aren't talking about it. I don't know why, but my half-sister and parents aren't talking to me either. I like the quiet, but my mother continues to call me in the early morning hours to go and get her at the bar. My father cooks his own meals, my mother cooks for her and my half-sister. I've become a master of making cereal, sandwiches, and canned soup. I also am very good at toast and scrambled eggs.

I'm spending more time by myself at the river. It's not the same as the woods. Trains are nearby, and they're loud and come by often. There are barges and different types of boats going up and down the river. It's not what I want, but it's all that I have. There is no more canvas bag to keep my things. I'm having trouble trying to find something that works. I try to keep things in a wooden box, but something chews through the box and rips up the blankets I have in there. I try using a duffel bag, but the same thing happens. I eventually discover an old tin milk box. It seems to be working okay. I find spending nights at the river stressful. There are rats, mice, and other creatures roaming around at night. When you combine that with the train and the traffic sounds from a nearby bridge, it is a place I think I can only go to only during emergencies.

Tommy and his older brother show up down at the river one day and begin to build a treehouse. They build a good place to stay. We all spend nights in the treehouse. It's comfortable and away from the creatures and things happening on the ground. This is a time of being around a fire at night and sleeping in the treehouse. All of this changes during a bad storm. We all go down to the river to be in the treehouse and discover the tree is on its side. The treehouse is in pieces. Tommy and his older brother begin making plans to build another one the next year. I'm asked to help them, and I agree. The treehouse was a great place to go before the storm destroyed it.

It's a Saturday when I come home from playing in a pony league game. I see my mother, and she won't look at me. When I ask where my half-sister is, she begins swearing and yelling at me. Tears are streaming down her face as she goes into her bedroom and slams the door. My mother later emerges from her bedroom a few minutes later and heads down the front stairs. I know she's going to a bar. When my father comes home, I ask him about my half-sister. He tells me she left for the Army that morning. I never knew the day or time she would leave. I know I should feel bad about not saying goodbye to her, but I don't. Our entire lives, she's been told she's my mother's daughter and I am my father's son. We never really spent much time together. Maybe I'll miss her someday.

My mother's drinking no longer takes place just in the evening. She goes to the bars at all hours of the day. I came home from school to get a call from her at the bar to go and get her. In my world this is good. It means she'll sleep until the next day and I'll have a rare opportunity to sleep through the night.

There is a time when I'm on my way back from baseball practice and passing a bar. I look inside to see my mother through a window. She is getting overly affectionate with a man. That night there is no call; she doesn't come home. My mother is gone a few nights a week. I have no idea where she is going. I suspect she's with the man from the bar. A guy from the baseball team who knows my mother asks if the guy he saw her with is my father. He doesn't look like the man who has dropped me off at practice. I don't know what to say. I quickly change the subject and leave.

One day, I'm coming home from playing in a pony league game. I get a call from my mother to come and get her at the bar. It's late in the afternoon, and she's very drunk. She is hanging on to me and spouting nonsense as I try to guide her to the apartment. Then the worst possible thing happens. A group of guys from the baseball team are on the other side of the street. They wave to me and I wave back. They ask if that's my mother and I nod my head in the positive. The group of them laugh at me as I walk with my drunken mother holding onto me.

The next few games are horrible. They won't stop taunting me about my mother. During the last game, the coach's son throws a batting helmet at me when I'm not looking. It hits me in the back of the head and knocks me down. He says something about my drunk mother and starts laughing. I'm on him with a flurry of punches. The coach comes over and breaks up the fight and tells me to leave, I'm done, I'm off the team. I'm not even given a ride back to the apartment. It's a very long walk.

The tendrils of hate begin to travel deeply into my being. I spend more time away from the apartment. My father doesn't seem to care what is going on with me or my mother. He simply goes to work in the morning, comes back to the apartment when he's done, goes into his room, closes the door, and watches television.

His routine is consistent. In the summer on the weekends, he plays golf. On the weekends in the winter, he goes to a veterans club to be with his friends. Early each Saturday morning he buys groceries and does the laundry at a laundromat. He never asks for help and seems to never notice anything going on in the apartment. I try not to disturb him.

I find my mother's boyfriend vile. He is crude, ignorant, and stupid. He tries to talk to me when my mother needs to be taken back to the apartment, but I make it clear I want nothing to do with him. This makes him angry. He calls me some names and I call him some names. He grabs me, I break away and push him. He falls into a booth. After this happens, other guys in the bar grab me. The bartender and the bar owner break things up. I'm told to never go into the bar again. I say some rather unflattering things about the bar as I leave. I now have to meet my mother outside the bar when she wants to hang on to me as she staggers back to the apartment.

I'm walking down the street after recently leaving my spot down near the river. I walk past a gas station and I notice my mother's boyfriend talking to one of the town's policemen. The boyfriend waves to me and I ignore him. He calls to me to come over to him, and I keep walking. I hear some quick footsteps behind me, and when I turn around, the boyfriend is trying to talk to me. He tells me how he doesn't care if I don't like what is going on between him and my mother, and I need to stop acting like a jackass about it. He then holds out some money and asks for us to be friends.

I knock the money out of his hand. When I try to walk away, he quickly grabs my shoulder, turns me around, and hits me in the face. I charge him, knock him down, and I start hitting him in the face. We're both struggling and swearing. The next thing I know, something hard has hit me in the side. I'm on the ground and the local police officer grabs me by the shirt and pulls me up. He slams me against a telephone pole and starts yelling about how I'm going to juvenile hall for attacking an adult. He looks at my mother's boyfriend and asks him if he'd like me to be arrested or taught a lesson. He says a lesson would probably save the local policeman a lot of paperwork.

As the policeman holds me, my mother's boyfriend slaps me in the face several times as he swears at me. He then punches me in the stomach hard enough to knock the wind out of me. My mother's boyfriend then grabs my hair and my head is pulled back. He then tells me if I try something like this again, I won't go to juvenile hall, I'll go to a funeral home.

After this, he and the local policeman laugh. I'm thrown to the ground by the local policeman. He tells me to get out of there before he changes his mind and takes me to juvenile hall. I'm slowly getting my breath back and stand up. I'm trying to walk away, but my face hurts and my side hurts pretty badly. After taking a couple of steps, I turn back and give both of them the middle finger. The local policeman starts to come after me, and I start running as best I can. I can hear from behind me that I'm being called a few more names. I struggle to run away from them.

The next day my mother asks what happened to me. I tell her the story of what her boyfriend and the local policeman did to me. She tells me she's glad it happened and hopes I learned a good lesson about not fighting with adults. I want to scream that he hit me first, but I've learned that doesn't matter. The only thing that matters is the feeling of being connected to the person who starts the fight. Those who have this connection will not believe the person they care about could have done anything wrong. I find it difficult to not let the hate I'm feeling for my mother consume me.

During the next few weeks, my mother's behavior gets worse. She leaves the front door open, and twice, drunk strangers come up the front steps. The first guy I'm able to talk into leaving with no problem. The second guy keeps telling me he just wants a sandwich, and then he'll leave. When I refuse, he gets belligerent and tells me I am going to make him a sandwich, or he will beat me up. I start yelling at him and my father comes out of his bedroom and starts yelling at the drunk guy and tells him to leave. My father threatens to call the police. The drunk man leaves and almost falls down the steps. Things are getting dangerous for us.

In the middle of the night, I smell smoke. I go down to the bathroom and the bathroom trash can is on fire. I pick it up, put it in the bathtub, and turn on the water. My father comes out and asks what's happening. I explain it and it appears my mother had put a lit cigarette in the bathroom trash can. My father has had it. He says we need to move away from the bars or my mother will get us killed.

My mother goes through a time when she doesn't go to the bar and slows down her drinking. She seems more sad than usual. I hear her talking on the telephone, and it appears her boyfriend has broken up with her. She blames me and feels I always ruin everything good in her life. She can't believe I attacked her boyfriend. My mother wonders if I should be sent to juvenile hall. I think about leaving the apartment, but I decide to confront her when she gets off the phone.

I call her some choice names and tell her how she disgusts me. I ask what kind of mother acts like she does with men in bars and expects her son to put up with it. My mother yells that she hates me and my father is no better. She then goes into her bedroom and slams the door. I know she's upset, but I don't care.

As I grow up, my parents often live in separate homes. During their entire time together, my parents never divorce or are legally separated. They just live apart from one another from time to time. When this happens, there is a routine. My father often comes to pick me up on certain weekends. Sometimes we go to arcades, to a pond to feed the ducks, or to a movie theater. One thing that always happens after we're done having fun is we go to a bar.

My time at the bar often consists of me sitting in a booth at the bar by myself. I'm given a bag of potato chips and a bottle of soda and told to occupy myself. My father then disappears. When I get bored, the bartender will let me sit in the back room and watch cartoons on a television away from the adults. My father will suddenly reappear after a time that seems to always be too long. He doesn't say anything to me. He simply drinks beer at the bar, smokes some more, and then takes me home.

One time, the owner comes into the bar from the back room. She is a woman about my father's age and dressed rather nicely. Her hair seems a bit messed up. A few minutes later my father also comes into the bar through the back room. His shirt is untucked.

I point to him and say, "Dad, your shirt is untucked."

My dad laughs after looking at his shirt and says, "You're right. I guess I need to fix it."

The owner of the bar and the other people around my dad begin laughing. I have no idea what is so funny. It isn't until years later that I realize what was happening during all those times at the bar. Decades later, my dad smiles when I ask him about it. He simply says I need to understand that a man has needs. I tell him so does a young child, and I walk away from him.

CHAPTER 9

A New Residence

My half-sister does not do well in the Army. She quickly becomes an alcoholic and tries to commit suicide. After some rather difficult times, she marries a man who is also in the Army. He's a soft-spoken person. Once I meet him, I can tell he's got a gentle spirit and a strong mind. He is dedicated to my half-sister. Soon their first child is on the way. My half-sister gets an honorable discharge from the Army after getting pregnant. Her total time served in the Army is less than two years. She seems to be happy.

My mother blames the problems experienced by my half-sister on living in the same household as me and my father. I'm so tired of the things she says, I no longer have the desire or will to argue with her. My desire to avoid her yelling, screaming, and throwing things is something I feel daily. There is no reason to attempt to be honest and tell her the truth. There is too much repercussion from it.

We eventually move away from the crappy apartment. We move into a new residence in the top half of a large house. It sits on a residential street. My dad can now park his car in a driveway. On the second floor is a large living room, a dining room that is my mother's bedroom, a kitchen, and a bathroom. On the third floor is where my father and I have our bedrooms. There is also a spare room with a sink. An older woman lives on the first floor and in the back of the house. There is another apartment on the first floor and tenants regularly come and go there. The street is quiet. I no longer have to worry about drunks coming in the middle of the night to try to break into our home. The house has a large front porch. My father enjoys sitting on it during the warm months of the year and reading the evening newspaper. Sometimes he drinks beer as he sits on the front porch. There are other times when he just sits and says hello to people walking past. I no longer have to hear the sounds of cars and people going in and out of stores, people arguing on sidewalks, people going in and out of a restaurant, or the sounds of people in bars. Things are getting better.

It is a long walk for my mother to get to a bar. She still does it, and getting up in the early morning hours to go and get her takes even more time. Her time spent drinking in bars decreases. My mother does what she always does and eventually is told to leave the closest bar to our house. She is told to not return.

My pregnant half-sister comes for a visit with her new husband, and they go to a bar with my mother. My half-sister has changed. She has been away from our family for over two years. My half-sister looks at my mother differently. She is no longer the mindless obedient girl who does whatever my mother asks of her. What would have been acceptable behavior from my mother before my half-sister left is no longer tolerated. My mother gets angry at my half-sister and says some mean things. The visit of my pregnant half-sister and her husband is cut short, and they leave a few days early. My mother is furious and blames me and my father. We both ignore her.

My mother begins to slowly change after this happens. Her trips to the bar decrease significantly. She begins to cook dinner for me and my father. My mother then tries attending a church that is a walk away from where we live. She wants me to go, but I refuse. My last church experience was not positive.

I'm nine years old and it's the first time my mother has left. I have no idea why she is no longer in the house. I'm told that she is away visiting relatives. She is busy visiting relatives for over a year.

A neighbor talks to my father, and they decide I need to get some love in my heart. I must go to church on Sunday. It's decided I'll be taken for a service at a Catholic church. This is the first time I've ever been in any church. I have no idea what to expect.

On a Sunday, the family pulls up to our house in a big, shiny Cadillac. I get inside and sit next to a kid my age. He doesn't respond when I try to talk to him. I ask why he won't talk to me; he whispers it's best to be quiet in his grandpa's car on Sundays. I'm wearing nice clothes and the men are wearing suits and the women are wearing nice dresses. We slowly make our way to the church.

It is a really large and clean place. There is a container with a sponge on it outside the room where people are going. Everyone takes their hand, touches the sponge, and then touches their face. I figure it's a place to wash your hands. When I try to pick up the sponge to wash my hands, the grandfather who brought me there hits me in the head and tells me not to be stupid. He then tries to explain what I'm supposed to do and I'm still confused.

There are a lot of people bowing, putting their hands all over their faces, and saying stuff I don't understand. I sit on a long wooden bench that isn't too comfortable. A guy standing in front the wooden benches is wearing fancy robes. He starts talking and I have no idea what he is talking about. There comes a time when the guy in the front motions for all the children to come to the front. We have to kneel for some reason, and then they give us these little round things to eat. I tell myself this isn't much of a snack and ask for another one. The kid next to me tells me I'm an idiot and to shut up. When I go back to the uncomfortable benches, the grandfather hits me in the head again. He tells me I need to just be quiet and do what every other kid is doing. I look around at all the other kids. They seem to be pretty miserable. I think I am doing exactly what the other kids are doing.

The kid who sat next to me on the car ride is standing with someone he knows after all the stuff happening in the big room is over. I ask him where a water fountain is. These two look at each other and smile. They point to this woman who is wearing a big black and white hat on her head that goes down to the dark clothes she's wearing. They tell me to ask her for a drink of the water from the jar she's holding. I do just that and the woman in the big black and white hat gasps. She is upset with me. The grandfather notices what is happening, comes over, and tries to hit me in the head again but I move. He then holds me and hits my behind. The grandfather tells me I have a lot to learn before I can be considered civilized.

I'm asked if I want to go home or if I want to go to their place for lunch. I tell them I want to just go home. I'm told how wonderful the lunch is that they have planned. My head hurts and the grandfather's cigar smoke is bothering me. I ask for them to please take me home. When we get to my house, the minute they stop, I'm out of the car, and I run as fast as I can into my house.

My father comes out to talk to them. After they leave, my father wants to talk to me. I'm told I need to learn to behave if I'm ever going to be permitted to be in a church again. My father tells me I embarrassed him today. He doesn't understand what I have to be upset about. I don't care. I keep telling myself how I'll never go to church again.

The next Sunday my father tells me I need to get ready to go to church. I hide in the attic. My father keeps going around the house calling my name. I don't move. He looks around the house but can't find me. I come out about an hour after the people in the Cadillac leave. When I come down, my father is furious with me. I tell him I don't want to go to church. He asks me why, and I tell him my head hurts from the grandfather hitting me. My father doesn't believe me. He then tells me not to go but I need to remember he tried to get me to church. I then experience a huge wave of emotional relief.

I realize my mother has been trying to change since we moved to the new house. I struggle to care about her attempting to change. I stay away from the house more than I am in it. She spends a lot of time in bed claiming she's sick. I come home one Saturday afternoon, and there's an ambulance in front of the house. My mother is on a stretcher and is being taken away. I later learn my mother has a serious case of diabetes.

When my mother returns from the hospital, she is not doing well with her diagnosis. She tries to continue drinking beer and ends up back in the hospital. After the second time, she has learned her lesson. She changes her diet, takes medication, and loses weight.

When my mother tries to attend church, it doesn't go well. She doesn't want to study the Bible, say prayers unless it's part of the service, or discuss anything about this religion. The reality of her church attendance is based on her desire to have a social group to replace the one she lost by no longer being able to go to a bar. The people at the church don't seem to understand her, and she doesn't seem to understand them. As my mother's attendance slowly dwindles, she spends more time by herself. The local library is a short walk away, and she goes there regularly to borrow books.

My mother has stopped yelling and screaming at me. She no longer swears at me or throws things. When I mention what she has done in the past, my mother tells me she doesn't know what I'm talking about. She refuses to deal with her feelings of shame and embarrassment from her behavior. On some level, I do feel bad for my mother. Her life of drinking in the bars and regularly getting drunk is over, and her daughter is now on her own, starting a family many miles away. My half-sister no longer tolerates my mother's bad behavior. My mother has no relationship with me or my father. I imagine my mother feels pretty alone.

I try to call my friend Tommy on the phone for a few weeks after the move. There is never any answer. I don't see him in school. I go to his apartment, knock on the door, and nobody seems to ever be home. I don't know what to do about it. A neighbor at Tommy's apartment building sees me. She comes into the hallway and tells me the upsetting story about Tommy's family.

It seems his father came home drunk a few weeks earlier and his mother called the police. When the police arrived, Tommy's father was hitting all the children as well as their mother. He was completely out of control. When the police tried to calm him down, he attacked them. Tommy's father fought with three local policemen. They eventually arrested him. Tommy's mother just left Tommy and his siblings the next day with no explanation of where she was going. Nobody knows where she has gone. Youth services were then called. Tommy and his siblings were all put in foster care. The neighbor is glad they're gone. I ask if she knows where they are right now, and she doesn't know and doesn't care. I miss my friend, but I'm getting used to only having friends for a short time. I will probably never see him again.

I no longer want to play baseball, so I join the Boy Scouts. I am friendly with the other kids, but we are very different. The times I go camping are enjoyable, but it is too structured, and I want to have the freedom to explore the woods on my own. Everybody wants to know where you are at all times. If I go into the woods, I need to go with other kids. If I go by myself, I'm given a time limit. Camping is done in a certain way and it is also very structured. My heart aches for a chance to just spend time in the woods alone, but I am not permitted. I feel like I'm looking through the glass of a store at my favorite chocolate cake. I can see it and smell it, but I can't have it.

I know most of the other scouts have been good kids their entire lives. They have very caring parents. They follow directions and do well in school. I find them boring. I can't relate to them. I still work hard and get just two levels away from the highly-coveted eagle scout rank. The troop I am in folds. The people in charge feel they're too old to do it anymore and nobody is willing to take their place. The other kids go to Boy Scout troops in other towns. I am finished with scouting. I don't think I can succeed at scouting or continue to enjoy it. I don't want to get too involved with something that makes me happy. Whatever I truly enjoy seems to leave me, get destroyed, or become horrible. If I get too happy with anything, there will come a time when it is ruined or taken away. It seems to always happen that way for me.

CHAPTER 10

The Myth of Nevada

It's the last day of school. I'm going to turn fourteen in the summer and for the first time that I can remember, I have no plans. A teacher in one of my classes has a big map of the United States on a wall. She asks kids in the class to come to the front of the room, point to a state on the map where they have been, and tell a story about it. I don't care about the extra credit points.

I think about telling the class about my time in California, but I don't think that's a good idea. I would be too ashamed and embarrassed to tell the class how my father got arrested and kicked out of our house. I don't want to tell how this caused my drunk mother to load me and my half-sister in a van, taking us to a bus station where we traveled on a bus for three days, then spent a few months in Sacramento before my father cut off my mother's money, and we had to come back.

The next thing I think about is telling the class about Nevada. My mother, half-sister, and father never discuss our time in Nevada. Any attempt to bring it up in conversation results in the subject being changed. If I persist, I'm told to stop and not bring it up again. My mother, half-sister, and father will leave a room or turn on the television or radio loudly to get away if I start talking about the Nevada trip. The hurt and anger associated with it never leaves my mother, father, or half-sister. I hadn't remembered it for a while until today.

They did talk about the Nevada trip with other people. A few times I heard my mother talk about it on the phone with her older children and friends. I heard my half-sister talk about it with her older siblings and friends. I know it happened, and why they don't want to talk about the trip with me I don't know. It was a time when I learned that wherever I go, no matter what happens, there are people who will be there to help me.

It's a few weeks after I start the fourth grade. I'm happy with my new clothes, pens, and notebook. My teacher seems nice, and I have a feeling school will be good this year.

In the middle of the night, my half-sister wakes me up. I'm told to get dressed. When I start to complain, I'm told a relative is sick and we have to go be with them. I ask which relative, my half-sister gives me a name, and I say I don't know that relative. She tells me to just hurry up, get dressed, and go downstairs.

I go downstairs, get on a coat, and go outside. We get into a car with a driver I don't know. The driver is a woman about my mother's age. I soon realize she is my mother's friend. As they talk, the driver keeps saying my mother is doing the right thing. She talks about never giving up on love and following your heart. None of this conversation makes any sense to me.

We get dropped off at a bus station. I'm given a suitcase and told to carry it. We get on a bus, and I notice our tickets say we're going to Reno, Nevada. I tell my mother I didn't know we had relatives in Nevada. I'm told to just be quiet. I sleep on the bus for a long time. When I wake up, I see long open prairies and soon that becomes desert. All the stops are places with people wearing cowboy boots and cowboy hats. I swear I see somebody who looks like John Wayne. I ask my half-sister if the relative we're going to see is a cowboy. She tells me to stop asking questions.

After a few days, we arrive in Reno, Nevada. A guy comes to greet us. My mother and this guy share a rather affectionate embrace, and my sister hugs the man and calls him dad. I don't know what to say. The man offers to shake my hand. After shaking his hand, I ask him his name. This is when I'm told this is my mother's second husband. This is my half-sister's father. I feel a little shocked and don't know what to say. I say it's nice to meet him. He tells me I can call him Ron.

We go to a hotel room. We stay there for a few days. We then go to a motel room that has a kitchen. It is in a small town. I tell my mother I want to explore the town. I'm told it's okay because she, Ron, and my half-sister want to spend some family time together.

I'm told not to go any further than around the block. I can't help myself because I'm fascinated by what I'm seeing. I see beautiful mountains in the distance. There is a desert area on the outside of the town. I walk past a store down the block from the motel that sells only cowboy hats, boots, shirts, pants, and belt buckles. I see some type of bush rolling through the parking lot. I later learn this is known as a tumbleweed. After walking a good distance, I look down a side street and see a corral with horses. People wearing western-style clothes are riding horses and spinning ropes. Next to the corral, there is a sign about learning how to be in a rodeo. I get lost. I quickly learn it is a small town. I walk a little longer and find our motel. When I come into the room, I see Ron, my mother, and half-sister in the kitchen area. Ron is playing a guitar. They don't seem to notice me. Ron isn't mean to me. He just gets annoyed if I talk to him too much or ask him questions. Everybody seems to be annoyed if I ask them questions.

After a few weeks in the motel, we move to a new trailer in a trailer park. I'm told I will be starting school after the weekend. I begin to wonder about my fourth-grade class back home. I think about the nice teacher. I have no idea what to expect. My half-sister and I haven't been in school for over a month.

On Monday my half-sister and I are standing at a location with other kids in the trailer park waiting for a school bus. Over half of them are Native Americans. The other kids talk among themselves and ignore us. When we get on the bus, it is an old bus. The ones back home were painted bright yellow with black stripes. This bus is yellow with black stripes but has paint chips on the outside and cracked windows. It is also dirty. As the bus moves out of the trailer park and onto the road, I wonder if the bus will make it to the school.

We get off the bus at the school and somebody from the school's office is waiting for us. The school is just one level with a flat roof. It's also old with paint chipping around its windows and doors. My half-sister and I are taken to the office by the person who greeted us. We take some tests, fill out some forms, and are then taken to the classrooms where we will be every day. The desks in the classroom are also old. This seems to be in keeping with the aesthetic standards of this particular Nevada educational system. After the teacher introduces me, I'm given a desk and some books.

I'm introduced to a girl who has the job of showing me around the school. She is a Native American, and I later learn she has the best grades in the class. After showing me around the school and informing me where to go for gym class, the location of the cafeteria, and more, she quickly leaves me. I ask why she is anxious to get away from me. As she's walking away the girl turns back and says she doesn't want anybody to see her alone with a white kid. I'm confused and don't know what to say.

I don't understand the classroom. Everything is so different from my old school. The kids in this class have been studying subjects for two months, and I'm completely new to them. The teacher is an older woman who doesn't like me and says something about people from back east. Her method of teaching is strange to me. If she calls on you to answer a question, and you don't get it right, she believes you weren't paying attention to what she was saying. You have to stand up. She then hits you on the behind with a yardstick. It doesn't hurt, but it does sting quite a bit. I'm so clueless about what is happening around me. The other kids and the teacher don't help me understand. I get questions wrong so often that when the teacher calls on me, I don't answer. I just stand up and await being hit with a yardstick. The kids in the class chuckle and the teacher is consistent; she always hits me with the yardstick.

Some kids sitting behind me think what is going on with me is wrong. Two brothers begin to help me. They explain things, and I begin to pass tests. I'm called on and I answer the questions correctly. They even help me with the confusing homework. Their family lives on the edge of town. I live too far away from them to walk to their house. I don't talk much to my half-sister's father. I try to ask him about being driven to visit my new friends at the edge of town. He ignores me. My mother tells me not to ask Ron anything like that again. I'm glad I have my own room in the trailer.

My mother, half-sister, and Ron often go away and forget to tell me. I get lonely and wander around the trailer park. I make friends with a boy about my age who is a Native American. He lives with his grandparents. Whenever they see me wandering around the trailer park, the grandparents tell me to come to their trailer. They give me food, let me watch their television, and spend time talking to me. They're happy people.

My friend and I often go out to an open piece of land against the trailer park that's a desert. I remember the day we were walking and I heard the sound of a rattlesnake. We could see it moving and watched its tongue moving in and out of its mouth. I told my friend this was just like the movies, and he laughed. He told me not to move. He then said something in his tribe's language to the snake. The rattling stopped, and the snake slowly moved away. My friend told me the snake was afraid. He said he told the snake to not be afraid. We were his friends and meant him no harm. I thought this was the greatest thing I've ever seen in my life.

Ron, my mother, and half-sister let me join them when they go to a rodeo. I think it is wonderful. Ron and my mother have been drinking. We walk past a booth selling cowboy attire. The man knows Ron and they begin talking and laughing. The man tells Ron he has to get a cowboy hat and boots for me. I stick out too much. They go back and forth, but I get a cowboy hat and boots. My half-sister doesn't want any cowboy items for some reason. I like them so much. I hate it when I have to take off my cowboy hat and boots.

I begin to make friends at school. One time a rather big kid comes up and starts pushing me. He starts saying I'm stupid and should go back east. I start pushing him back but the big kid looks at something behind me. He then turns and walks away. When I turn around, it's one of the brothers who helps me in class. He was standing behind me. I tell him I wasn't afraid of that kid. He tells me I should be afraid of him. He's not a nice kid. I'm asked if I want to go and play a game of kickball with him, his brother, and some other kids on the school playground. I tell him that would be great. The kickball game lasts the entire recess. I'm asked to join the brothers and spend time with them during every recess. I'm having a great time.

I'm starting to get comfortable with the routine of getting on the bus and going to and from school during the week. My Native American friend is one of the best friends I've ever had. He's teaching me more about the desert, and I pick up a few words of his Native American language. School is starting to make sense to me. I start fitting in with the other kids when I wear my cowboy hat and boots to school. Having the brothers as my friends keeps other kids from trying to push me around.

Things are not going well between my mother and Ron. He seems to be rejecting my half-sister. When Ron left my mother many years earlier, he married another woman and had children with her. Ron tells my half-sister about his kids. She's crushed when he talks about them. I don't know why, but I don't feel bad for her.

It's a Saturday and I have spent the day with my Native American friend and his grandparents. They are wonderful people. I go to sleep thinking about spending the next day exploring the desert with my friend. I'm woken up by my half-sister in the middle of the night. I'm told to get ready to go to town. I try to get dressed, but I can't find my cowboy hat and boots. I ask my mother about them, and she tells me to put on my tennis shoes and get ready to go. I do as she says because my mother seems extremely upset about something. We go out of the trailer in the dark and get into a taxi cab. The next thing I know we're at the bus station. My half-sister tells me we're going back. I start to cry and my mother grabs me by the shoulder. She says in my ear for me to quit being a baby and be a man. I'm told she's ashamed of my behavior.

On the first day of the bus ride. I'm numb to my emotions and can't feel anything. I constantly think about the school, the brothers, and my Native American friend and his grandparents. I want to go back to the desert and wear my cowboy hat and boots. I try not to cry when I realize it's all gone. I feel sad and alone.

The first day we get back to the farmhouse, my father starts arguing with my mother. After screaming at her and throwing some things, he goes to one of his veterans clubs. My mother purchased beer before we arrived. She and my half-sister spend the rest of the evening at the kitchen table. They ignore me and when my father comes home, he ignores me.

I'm really sad when I go out for a walk. I go to a housing complex. A family has put a canvas bag out for the trash. When I see it, I can't stop looking at it. A man sees me admiring the canvas bag and comes down his driveway to where I'm standing. He tells me I can have the canvas bag if I want it. I look inside and there is a wool blanket, a down blanket, and some books about baseball. I ask him if I can have those as well. He tells me I can have all of it. I thank him. I tell the man this means quite a bit to me. I'm told how this is what he took camping. It gives me ideas about spending time in the woods.

I never raise my hand in class and talk about my time in Sacramento or Nevada. My heart is still hurting from leaving both of them. I fear tears could start coming down my cheeks if I talk about it. One of the kids next to me asks if I've ever been outside of the state. I smile and tell him an easy lie. I say I've never been out of the state. He then tells me about his trips to Florida and Wisconsin to visit relatives. Another person talks about how their grandparents left them a house in North Carolina when they died, and they go there every year on vacation. I'm also told by a girl how her mother was born in Hawaii, and they go there every other year.

They all have such nice stories about going places with their families. I don't want to share my story. I'm ashamed and embarrassed by my family and the reason for our trips. I think nobody would understand. The other kids would be more convinced that I'm strange.

In Nevada, my mother had her heart broken again by a man who had broken it many years before. My half-sister had to experience the sting of rejection from her father. My father had to deal with deep feelings of betrayal. I'm glad when the last day of school is over. I know my family is not like most of the other kid's families. In my mind, it's something I've had to learn to accept.

CHAPTER 11

Consumed By Anger

As my fourteenth birthday approaches, I'm feeling angry. I don't understand it, but I'm angry all the time. My mother no longer drinks. My home is now quiet compared to when we lived in the crappy apartment. There is talk about what I want for my birthday. This means it will be remembered this year. My parents are making an honest effort to make things better. I keep telling myself I should be happy.

I'm tired of getting into fights. I avoid playing baseball. The other kids have teased me too much during school about my drunk mother. I don't like them, and I know they don't like me. The story of her hanging onto me as I guided her home is still talked about by the kids who saw it. If it gets mentioned by any of them when we play baseball, I don't know if I'll be able to hold back and not get into a fight. Then the coach will yell at me, and I might even get kicked off a baseball team for a second time. I figure it's best to avoid the trouble playing baseball could bring me.

I explore the area around the river during the summer. I get a little lost and decide to go to a group of houses I see in the distance. When I come out of the woods, I'm in a backyard. There are no fences. I'm walking toward the street when I hear a voice from behind me.

"Hey, asshole, what are you doing in my yard?"

When I turn around, it is a kid from school. His name is Derick. There are only two kids in school that scare me. Derick is one of them. He has blonde hair and blue eyes. Derick always smells of cigarette smoke and is constantly upset about something. I've seen him fight other kids, and he gets a scary look in his eyes when he's angry. The school's administrators don't know what to do with him. When Derick gets paddled, he laughs. The more they hit him, the more he laughs. I think some teachers are afraid of him.

"I was down by the river and got a little lost. I'm just trying to get to the street, so I can walk home," I say.

Derick yells, "You can't just walk through somebody's yard because you're lost. What kind of a stupid asshole are you?"

"Look, I am just trying to get to the street, so I can walk home. Leave it alone."

Derick then swears and runs at me. He yells about being able to legally defend his property against assholes like me. He pushes me, I push him back, and we're wrestling. I get him in a headlock and hit him. He laughs no matter how many times I hit him. This shocks me, and he gets out of my headlock. Derick then gives me a flurry of punches to the face. I try to cover myself but he keeps punching me. I then start punching back. I hit Derick in the mouth, and he starts bleeding. This only makes him laugh more. I'm getting scared. I realize he's not going to stop. I land another punch to his head and Derick staggers back laughing. Before I know what he's doing, Derick grabs a large rock and throws it at my head. I duck at the last moment and avoid it hitting me. Derick then runs at me and grabs me again. As we're wrestling, he is saying how much fun he's having. Derick tells me he's glad an asshole like me trespassed on his property. He gets some more punches to my side, and I go to the ground. On an impulse, I quickly grab a handful of dirt and throw it into his face. Derick covers his eyes and starts swearing. I start running. His eyes are filled with too much dirt to follow me. I don't stop running for a long time. It takes me quite a while to calm down. In my mind, Derick would not have stopped until one of us was seriously hurt or dead. It gets me extremely upset as I think about it.

A few weeks later, I'm at the playground when somebody tells me they need help delivering special edition newspapers. I have nothing going on that day, so I agree to help him. I'm told to knock on the door and hand the special edition newspaper to the person who answers it. If nobody answers the door, I am to simply leave it on their porch.

Everything is going well, until I knock on a door and Derrick answers. I have completely forgotten this was his house.

I hand him the newspaper and say, "Special edition newspaper."

Derick smiles and says, "I remember you."

He takes the newspaper and starts laughing. Derick asks if I want to come in, and I tell him no. I'm terrified. I'm about to start running for my life.

"Why don't you come back later, and we can pick up where we left off last time you were here? That was a lot of fun."

I reply, "I don't think so."

I turn and start walking away. I can hear Derrick behind me laughing. He's yelling that I'm nothing but a trespassing asshole who needs to be taught a lesson. I then hear his front door slam shut. I feel so much relief my knees almost buckle.

This is the summer I begin to realize many things. I have no control over the past, but the people in the town where I live are determined to let the past control their view of me. The past determines their thoughts and attitudes toward me. Nobody realizes I'm doing better in school and my mother is no longer a drunk. Her hanging on to me in the early morning hours to guide her home has stopped. I'm still thought of as a bad kid from a bad home. I feel trapped in people's perceptions of me.

During the middle of the summer, my mother leaves to go and spend time with my half-sister and her new grandchild. She doesn't give a return date. My mother is gone helping my half-sister for a few weeks. This is when people ask where my mother is, I tell them my half-sister just had a baby and my mother is visiting her. After I say this, some people simply look at me and smile. Others make sarcastic comments. I slowly understand these individuals refuse to believe what I've told them is the truth. They're content to believe things are no different from the way they were in the past. I'm told by a neighbor that it's a shame my parents don't want me. I yell at one person who tells me to calm down and not to be upset. She says my mother has left my father several times before and might stay gone this time. They then add that if she comes back, she'll just do it again. I realize my father has told too many people too much about our family's past.

I hear my father arguing with my mother on the phone a month after she left. He's yelling at her, and I can hear her yelling back at him on the other end of the line. He tells my mother to not come back. He hangs up the phone and walks past me. A few days later, he sends a trunk filled with my mother's things to my half-sister's address. I'm so angry at both of them. I begin to believe that the ideas about me and my family from the people in this town are correct. I now think nothing will ever change, and I feel defeated.

Now, I'm so angry, I don't care about anything. I figure I'm never going to be considered a good kid, so maybe I need to show the world how much of a bad kid I can become. This is when I start shoplifting for the first time since we came back from Sacramento. I get candy, baseball hats, and even a radio. None of it means anything to me. I never get caught. A few guys from the playground ask where I got things, so I tell them how I stole them from stores. They seem to believe it's a simple thing to do. A few of them try shoplifting and get caught. I'm not surprised.

I meet a kid who recently moved to the town. His name is Reggie, and his family is as messed up as mine. We instantly become friends. I show him around the town and tell him about things happening in the different neighborhoods. I think of the time

Tommy did this for me, and I miss him. Reggie's family moved here after living in the big city about twenty miles away. He knows a lot of things.

Reggie shows me how to break into cars and take the tape decks and anything else of value. We then take the stolen items and meet a guy Reggie knows. This guy gives us money for the things we've stolen from cars. We're making good money doing this. Reggie also shows me how to take a hammer and break open parking meters. Between these two criminal acts, we are making quite a bit of money. The next thing Reggie teaches me is how to break into train cars when the train is stopped. The first time we do this, Reggie says to hide the things we take from the train car in the bushes near the train tracks. The guy Reggie knows drives to a point near the railroad at night with a van. We load everything we've stolen from the train onto the van. The guy gives us quite a bit of money. I laugh when I think about some teachers at school. They want students to try to decide what skills they have for their future. I want to tell them I'm an excellent criminal.

Things are very good for a long time. I go home one day, and my father is screaming for me to come upstairs. He is as furious as I've ever seen him. It appears the police have called, and I have to go to the police station. When we arrive, I see Reggie. He's all smiles. Reggie comes over and whispers in my ear to say nothing and not mention the guy to who we gave all the stuff. If I don't do this, he's not responsible for what happens to me.

I don't say anything. The police are angry. My father tells me to plead guilty to the charges. I tell him I'm not saying anything. He tells me if I don't, I can't live in his house anymore. He doesn't care what happens to him or me right now. I'm tired of him screaming at me. I agree. I'm taken to juvenile hall for a few weeks. I am then permitted to go to my home and am put on three months' probation.

Reggie's family seems to know how the system works. They get an attorney. Reggie is never taken to juvenile hall and gets off with a month of probation. Neither of us mentions the guy or the money we got from him. I realize this is the end of my career as a criminal. I never want to experience being arrested again. Reggie keeps on doing criminal things and is angry when I no longer want to join him. A threatening note is left on the front door of my house for me. It's from the guy Reggie and I have been giving the stolen items. I tell Reggie if I don't say anything about him when I'm arrested and locked up in juvenile hall, why would I say anything now? Nobody is asking me about him, and I'm serving my punishment. Reggie says this is between me and the guy. I ask Reggie to pass on to him what I've just said. Reggie says he'll think about it. I never get a threatening note again. Reggie completely fades out of my life in a short time.

This has been a summer where I've changed. I realize my anger could destroy me if I let it. I need to decide my future. My parents' problems have had a grip on me for too long. I need to look past them. My grades have never been good, but they are better now than they ever have been in the past. I realize I'll never be able to go to college. I have no mechanical abilities, so anything associated with using numbers or tools is also out for me. I feel lost.

I spend a lot of time alone trying to stay out of trouble. When finishing my school work, I wonder if working hard will matter for me. I'm walking down a sidewalk towards the end of summer. I see a kid from school playing the guitar. I'm fascinated. I ask him about it. He tells me where he got his guitar and where he takes lessons.

I tell my father I am going to get a guitar. He agrees to pay for lessons. I have a brand-new expensive guitar and tell my father I bought it off of a friend. He never questions what I tell him. I don't think he wants to know where I got the money for it. Lessons don't go well. The guitar teacher is rather obnoxious to me. He yells at me, I yell at him, he grabs my guitar, and I kick over his music stand. I'm told to leave. This is the end of my musical tutelage. A friend shows me musical books with instructions. I get some of these books and learn to play a few songs. I don't know much about playing the guitar other than how to imitate what I see in pictures. It's enough, and I'm satisfied.

My father buys me a ten-speed bike for my birthday. I'm really happy. I'm so surprised he remembered my birthday. I spend most of the remaining summer days riding it everywhere. A neighbor comes by and suggests I go and be on the football team. My father thinks it's a great idea. I figure I'll never be an academic, a musician, a baseball player, and I no longer want to be a criminal. Football may be something worth trying.

<h1 style="text-align:center">CHAPTER 12</h1>

A World of Words

My experience on the football team lasts only one season. I initially think it will replace my desire to play baseball, but I quickly learn they are two very different sports. I'm not good at running and remembering formations. The only thing I enjoy is the physical contact. I'm not good at blocking, but I am one of the best when it comes to tackling. The coach says he'll work with me to improve my speed, so I can chase down ball carriers better. During the season, I am on the special teams. I don't complain. I'm glad I'm able to play the game.

I work hard and improve. The other kids on the football team have their different cliques. The starters are in one group. The kids who have been playing football in a league near their home for years are in another group. I don't fit in with any of them. The other players aren't mean or obnoxious. They're just focused on enjoying the experience with the friends in their clique. I don't want to talk too much with anybody. I'm afraid the conversation will become about families. I don't want to talk about my family or anything going on with us. The other players don't notice me too much. It's not a bad time.

We have a lousy season. Nobody blames anybody, and I have a sense the players just want to have fun playing football. By the time the last game of the season arrives, the players aren't taking anything too seriously. They're glad for it to be over. The starters are taken out by the second half of the last game. I'm put in to play linebacker to start the second half. I'm doing okay.

Things had been going well for me all season. I believe they don't know or don't care about my family. It's a shock to me when a player from my team suddenly wants to tease me during the fourth quarter of the last game. He's sitting on the bench and yells for me to get the quarterback like I'm going to a bar to get my drunk mother. The other guys on the bench around him laugh. I'm furious.

The next play is one where the other linebackers and I rush the quarterback. When the play starts, the guys on the line do their job and create a hole. I'm through the line and on the quarterback before he knows it. He tries to back up, but I put my helmet down, ram it into his groin, and wrap my arms around his legs. I pick him up and then run a few steps before I slam him down on the ground hard.

I hear officials' whistles and players for the opposing team are on me. I see fists coming at me and feel kicks. Coaches from both sides are on the field trying to get players to stop fighting. I'm thrown out of the game. An official tells me a football field is no place for someone who plays dirty like me. It's a home game. The coach tells me to go to the locker room and go home. When I'm walking away, I hear someone say they know the magic words that will turn me into a lunatic. Then I hear the laughter.

No matter how much I think things are forgotten, I realize they'll always be remembered. I'm never going to fit in with the kids with nice homes or the ones who have been going to school here since kindergarten. I decide that it's best I don't fit in with them. I begin to realize my family history will follow me wherever I go in this town. No matter how much I try to forget the pain of the past, there will be someone who remembers it. Some people will try to use it against me.

My time playing football ends there. I almost play for half of a game. I have the distinction of being the only player from the team to have been thrown out of a game for as long as anyone can remember. This is the end of my high school athletic career.

My mother returns after being gone for several months. She and my father immediately begin fighting. My mother acts like I don't exist and doesn't even acknowledge I'm around for a few days. She is too busy being on the phone complaining to her friends and older children about my father. When she isn't doing this, she is spending time at the homes of her friends. They don't drink. They just smoke cigarettes and complain. Every day I leave early in the morning. My daily goal is to spend as little time as possible in the house.

It's summer and I'm always busy riding my bike or going to the river bank and exploring it. I know I'm looking for something in life that makes sense to me. I'm tired of being in trouble. When school starts, I realize I have no friends and no desire to have any. As I walk around school, I see other kids who are loners like myself. They're quiet and stay to themselves. One of the classes I hate the most is gym. I'm always picked last for a team. When we play a game, I'm just as good as any of the other kids. I realize the popular kids and especially the ones from the football team just don't think much of me. This makes me dislike them even more. We stay away from one another. This is acceptable to me. I just want to be left alone. I now try to avoid any situation where I could lose my temper.

A big change happens in my life. It comes in the form of discovering my ability to make sarcastic comments about everything. Kids sometimes hear what I'm saying and laugh. I get pretty good at it. During English class, a teacher thinks I'm not paying attention. She asks me what we're studying. I tell her a play by Bill Shakespeare called *The Merchant of Venice*. The teacher tries to correct me and says his name is William. I ask her why? I point to a kid in our class who is named Bill. I say his name is William, but we call him Bill. So why can't we call the play's writer Bill Shakespeare?

Other kids in the class laugh. Some pile on and want to know the answer to the question. The teacher sighs and simply says that he is always referred to as William Shakespeare. I say then it's not actually wrong to refer to him as Bill. The teacher reluctantly agrees but says in her class he will be referred to as William Shakespeare. I ask the teacher if this means we can call him Bill Shakespeare outside the classroom. She is angry now and tells me she doesn't care what I do outside the classroom.

I speak softly so only those around me can hear. I say, "Outside the classroom, I like to spend my time studying Bill Shakespeare."

There is laughter. The teacher asks what I said. I tell her that I'm encouraging my fellow students to read the assigned play. She is angry and tells me to stop it. This is when she begins speaking about our homework and the lesson starts. I don't understand why I'm so happy.

After the Bill Shakespeare incident in class, I'm instantly a hit with some of the other kids. I realize it's possible to express anger at a school system without doing anything physical. Sarcasm is much easier and doesn't involve getting in a fight or facing a painful punishment. It also causes other kids to laugh and like you. The Bill Shakespeare incident causes me to have an epiphany. It changes the way I look at life. Sarcasm is the only thing since baseball that comes easily to me. It's not something other kids can do well. I now begin to feel that not being like the other kids is a good thing.

I make friends with a kid named Neil. He is small and wears glasses. Neil has never liked sports. He is really fun and knows quite a bit about books and movies. I don't tell him about my family's history, and I hope he never learns about my criminal past. When I'm with kids from good homes, I'm always so ashamed and embarrassed about my family and my past. I will lie about it if necessary. I hate being judged on things that happened when I was younger and can't change.

I'm invited to Neil's house and have a great time. When sitting in his bedroom and talking, I notice some magazines on writing. I ask him about them, and he tells me how he sold a joke for $1.50 to some company he found in one of the magazines. I'm stunned at what I'm hearing. I sound so unintelligent when I ask him if people actually do make money from writing words. He laughs and tells me that book authors get paid, people who write for magazines get paid, and people who write for newspapers get paid. I ask how much they get paid. Neil laughs when I just stare at him. I'm thinking about how I could write something sarcastic and get paid for it. If people laugh when I say sarcastic things, maybe someone will pay me when I write sarcastic things. We spend the rest of the time talking about making money with writing. Neil gives me a few old copies of his writing magazines. He tells me to take them home because he's done with these magazines and was going to just throw them away. I almost can't control my excitement.

I get home and start reading the magazines from cover to cover. I make notes in the margins and underline things. I read about famous writers as they discuss their paths to success. I'm fascinated to learn of the many ways some people make money with writing. They do everything from writing slogans for buttons to writing movies, press releases, short stories, poems, technical books, school books, greeting cards, jokes, and more. My mind almost can't take in all the possibilities.

I look at the section of each magazine where people are willing to pay money for certain types of writing. They all expect the stories sent to them to be typed. I don't have a typewriter. I keep telling myself I will one day and when that day arrives, I need to be ready. Purchasing notebooks is something I can afford. I get some notebooks, as well as new pens, and begin filling them with my writing ideas.

When I start writing stories, it is almost like a drug. I'm taken on long journeys to a universe of my imagination. I can control every aspect of the universe as it is a world of my creation. In school, nobody seems to bother me when I'm writing in my notebooks, not even teachers. I suspect everyone thinks I'm doing school work.

My mother comes into my bedroom when I'm busy working on a story. She sees the writing magazines and asks about them. I begin to tell her about the world of writing that I've discovered. I explain how my friend Neil got paid $1.50 for a joke.

She laughs and says I'm not that smart. She tells me this is something done by people with an education who are intelligent. My mother reminds me of the times I've been in trouble in school, gotten arrested, and my poor grades. She tells me I'm too much like my father. I need to get a menial job like him or go into the military.

According to her, I need to accept that a kid like me with my past doesn't have too many options in life. She thinks I should worry more about finding ways to not go to jail when I get older.

When she leaves, I refuse to let myself give up on writing. I'm so angry. I have an urge to go and destroy things. I tell myself I have to ignore my mother's words. I am now a man of words. The next thing I know, I'm writing a story about an evil mother who controls the innocent population of a planet. The only one who can stop this woman's destructive ways is her heroic son. They have a battle and the mother is destroyed by her son with a silver ball that explodes when he throws it at her.

I feel better after writing this story. I calm down. After this, when my mother upsets me, I read this story. I sometimes add to the story and make the exploding mother scene more graphic.

It is a nice day and my father is on the front porch when I'm on my way back from the store. He says he wants to talk to me. When I sit down, he tells me he knows about the writing magazines. He doesn't want me to get my hopes up about this stuff. My father explains how we're just working people. College isn't something for people like us. He thinks I should go into an advanced shop class and learn a trade. My father tells me all the wonderful things about learning a trade.

I tell him I'm not good with numbers or tools. I have no mechanical ability for anything. I remind him how I can't fix things and find helping him when he works on his car beyond boring. I barely pass the required shop classes. I don't understand what they're trying to teach me in those classes. Any attempt by me to take an advanced shop class would result in me failing it in a big way.

My father reminds me of my bad grades, getting arrested and suspended, and the trouble I've gotten into during school. I'm angry. I yell that I'm not going to learn a trade because I can't do it. He asks me what I plan to do when I'm on my own. I tell him I plan to not live in this house with him and my mother. That's all I care about right now. My father tells me he's only trying to help. The past created by my parents caused me so many problems and is now being used as a weapon against me to try to get me to give up on my dream. I'm angry. I tell him he's helping me like an iceberg helped the Titanic. We're both quiet for a moment. The sinking of the Titanic is something we just learned about in history class. I can now be sarcastic without even thinking about it. I tell myself I've just invented auto-sarcasm speak. I like it.

I leave my father and go up to my bedroom. I close the door and write down what just happened in one of my notebooks concerning the invention of auto-sarcasm speak. The more I look at it, the more I like it. My parents are right about my past behavior, but I tell myself I don't care. I just enjoy the experience of writing stories in my notebooks. Nothing else matters to me right now.

CHAPTER 13

Girls Look Different

Soon it's summer, and I have nothing planned. My parents and I don't go on a vacation like the other families on the block. We don't have a cabin in a rural part of the state or relatives living in other states we plan to visit. I'm done with sports as well as being a criminal. I think my summer will involve spending time at the local library writing stories and trying to figure out how to get a typewriter. I ask for one for my fifteenth birthday, but my father says it may be too expensive. I consider going back to a life of crime, but it is an idea that lasts only a few seconds.

My body is changing. I'm big enough that when my mother tries to hit me, I just grab her hand and push her back. I think she knows the days of hitting me just because she's frustrated with something to do with my father are over. My mother tries to play it off as if she only means it as a joke. When I look at her, she understands I know that's a lie.

On a warm day, I notice a girl I assume to be around my age walk past our house. I've never seen her in school. She has red hair, blue eyes, freckles, and I can't stop looking at her. My throat goes dry, and my heart rate increases when I see her. I don't know how to handle it, but I'm embarrassed by this feeling. I go onto our porch the same time the next day just to see her.

When the girl with the red hair walks by, she looks at me and says, "Hello."

My throat goes dry and I struggle to say, "Hello."

I want to say more, but I just watch her walk away. I'm angry with myself for not saying more. I plan to do better the next day.

In the morning, I look in the mirror. I make certain my hair is brushed and the few patches of hair on my face are shaved. I put on a nice shirt. This time, I'm not going to simply sit on the porch. I'm determined to walk down the street and talk to her. I go over possible conversations and practice in the mirror. I plan to tell her I've lived in places out west. She may be one of these people who have never left the state. That should impress her.

The girl with the red hair comes down the street.

She notices me and says, "Hello."

I say, "Hello, hope you're having a good day."

She smiles and says, "It's warm and the sun is shining. Isn't it a beautiful day?"

I agree, and she continues walking to the house down the street. I know which house she left yesterday. There is a spot at the end of the block. I position myself there and wait. After waiting for her to emerge at the same time as yesterday, the girl with the red hair comes out of the house, down the steps, and onto the sidewalk. She starts walking, and I walk behind her. This is it. This is my big moment. I plan to find out her name and get to know her. I tell myself this has to happen.

I hurry my pace and get next to her and smile.

She smiles back and says, "I see you every day on your porch. What's your name? My name is Tanya."

I clear my throat and try to say my name, but I struggle again and my throat is dry, I struggle some more.

I finally say, "Mark."

The next thing I do is try to say something else. I stutter, I get frustrated. I suddenly yell, "Ah, screw it."

I then begin hurrying toward my house. Tonya calls me to come back to her. I slowly walk back with my head down.

She looks at me and says, "There is no reason to get upset. I don't bite. It's okay. How about you walk with me to where my mother works? She's going to take me home."

I feel as light as a feather. I soon learn that Tanya is an older woman. She's going to be seventeen this summer and will graduate this coming school year. Tanya is going to get her driving permit next month. She lives in another town and goes to another school.

I hear how her mother drives to work and drops Tanya off so she can be with her grandmother, since her grandfather is in the hospital. She gets her grandmother things from the store, cleans her home, and does other things to help out. I think Tanya is one of the most beautiful girls I've ever spoken to in my life.

Living in another town means Tanya knows nothing about my family. The stories of my mother, her drinking, and even my criminal past won't get to her. I feel as if Tanya won't be influenced by my parents' history. She can get to know me without knowing about those things. I'm really happy.

Seeing her is the highlight of my day. I decide to pick her some wildflowers. When I give them to her, Tanya smiles and tells me I'm so sweet. She gives me a little hug. Tanya tells me I should have a girlfriend because I'm so nice. I confess that I don't have a girlfriend. I want to say she is the one I want to be my girlfriend, but I'm too scared. That evening, I write stories about a young boy who is wealthy and can buy anything he wants for the red-haired girl of his dreams. The story takes up several pages. I read it and add to it daily.

My time with Tanya lasts a few weeks. When I talk with her, I'm as happy as I can remember ever being in my life. I dream of her when I don't see her. I can't get her out of my mind. I keep telling myself something will happen for her to be my girlfriend. I know it.

It's a sad day when my time with Tanya comes to an end. I am surprised and hurt, but when it happens, it's my fault. Tanya is walking away from her grandmother's home, and I'm walking with her, and we're talking. She tells me how her grandfather is back, and they no longer need her to come to see them every day. Tanya has a cousin who will now go to see them. My heart breaks.

The next thing I know a car stops beside us. The window is rolled down and a guy smiles at Tanya.

"Hey, how about you and I go and get some ice cream?"

Tanya looks at me and says loud enough for the guy in the car to hear, "This is my boyfriend Jack, I told you about. He thinks he's a big deal since he has his driver's license. He also makes a lot of money being a caddie at the golf course. Good thing he has me to keep him in line."

When she looks at the guy in the car, they exchange a laugh.

I'm devastated. Tanya did tell me she had a boyfriend the first day I talked to her. She has mentioned him several times since then. I didn't want to hear it. I didn't want to think about her having a boyfriend. The dream of her being my girlfriend is something I held onto tightly. I can't be angry because she has been honest with me. I feel empty inside.

The guy in the car says, "Who is this guy with you?"

Tanya says, "This is my friend Mark. He is one of the sweetest boys in this town."

The guy looks at me and says, "Hey, you can come with us for ice cream if you like. I'll treat."

I refuse. Tanya wants me to go since this is the last day she's going to be with her grandmother. She tells me it will be fun. I make up a quick lie and tell them I have to go do some work with my father. My father is actually out playing golf with his friends.

When Tanya gets in the car, she and the guy exchange a kiss before going down the road. I slowly walk home. I go up to my room and write a story about a young guy defeating an older guy in an intense battle for the hand of a beautiful red-haired girl. It's one of the stories that I show to no one but read on my own now and then.

I tell my friend Neil what happened. He has an interesting view of it. Neil says it sucks Tonya couldn't be my girlfriend, but it sucks that her boyfriend seems like such a nice guy. A nice boyfriend who drives and has a job. I completely agree with him.

A few days later I get caught in a thunderstorm, and I'm trying to make it home. A car pulls up, the window is rolled down, and it's Tanya's boyfriend Jack offering me a ride home. I get in and he takes me home. I wish I could dislike him. If he were some rogue who I needed to protect Tanya from, I'd feel much better. I hate him for being such a good person. It ruins everything.

Interacting with girls begins to take a more prominent role in the lives of me and my friends. Neil tells me he has a girlfriend. I ask him if he has ever kissed her, and he tells me not yet. They spend their time at her house working on paintings or watching movies. At his house, they listen to music and build models. Neil tells me he's going to try to hold her hand soon.

I meet up with Tommy's friend Roger. He and I spend a day down by the river just exploring. It appears he has a girlfriend in another town. He's done a lot more than just kiss her. She's a year older than him. Roger now feels he is quite the adult. He tells me how she has a friend that would be perfect for me. Feeling a bit insecure, I tell him I don't know about meeting her.

We eventually get to Roger's house. He doesn't live in a crappy apartment; his family lives in a crappy house. There are old, rusted cars on his lawn as well as an old washing machine and more. We go to his room, and Roger calls his girlfriend. I'm spending my time listening to the music on his record player and petting his dog.

He suddenly hands me the phone and says, "Why don't you talk to Jenny for a while?"

I'm scared about talking to a girl I don't know and have never seen. I mouth words saying I don't want to talk to her. Roger grabs my hand and puts the phone's receiver in it. He then points to the receiver and leaves his bedroom. I clear my throat. Jenny starts talking and wants to know if the things Roger says about me are true. She asks about my past. I ask her why she wants to know about it. I've never told Roger about going to juvenile hall or being arrested. I've just told him about some of the crimes I've committed. Jenny tells me the things I've done are so cool. I never thought being a criminal would get me anything but trouble, but it seems as if it just may have gotten me a girlfriend.

I don't want a girl to come to my house and meet my parents. My mother no longer drinks, but I still have no idea what she will say or do from one day to the next. I do know if, given the opportunity to embarrass me, it will be done by her. My father will have no problems teasing me, and the whole thing would be a nightmare.

Jenny wants me to come to her house. It's Saturday and my father is out playing golf. I tell her I'll be over around noon. Jenny asks me how I'll get to her house, and I tell her I'll hop a train. There is a train that goes toward where she lives right before noon every Saturday. I tell her I'll just hop on it and ride it to her house. She lives near the railroad tracks, so I figure it will be easy.

I don't think Jenny believes me. She laughs as she says, "Of course you will."

I make it to the railroad tracks, and the train is moving slowly down the tracks. I have never been on it as far as Jenny's house, but I'm not worried.

As I get closer, the train speeds up. I see her house in the distance. I see Jenny is outside in her yard. She has long blonde hair, blue eyes, and an amazing figure. Her father is standing next to her, cooking food on a grill.

I wave and hear Jenny say, "Dad, he's here, and look, he's actually riding a train."

The train is going faster than usual. I time my jump to get off it, but I go down when I hit the ground and roll a little in the dirt. I get up, dust myself off, and start walking to Jenny's house. Jenny is excited and waving at me. Her father is just standing behind his grill with a stunned expression on his face.

When I get to her house, Jenny puts her hand around my waist and introduces me to her father. I shake his hand. Jenny's father asks how often I hop on moving trains. I tell him only when it's necessary. Her mother comes out, and I am introduced to her. They try to hide it, but I know they're upset for some reason. Jenny tells her parents she is going to show me around.

The next thing I know we're in the woods. Jenny puts her arm around my neck and kisses me.

"Oh, you need some practice in the kissing department," she says.

We keep kissing. Then Jenny breaks away and leads me around paths in the woods.

I say, "Your father seems upset about me hopping a train to get here."

Jenny smiles and replies, "Oh, don't worry about him. That was one of the coolest things I've ever seen. You actually rode a train from your house all the way here. I mean, you jumped off, rolled in the dirt, and then just walked right up to my dad and said hello. Roger is right. You are one wild guy."

I want to tell her I feel like a dumb guy right now. Me jumping off a moving train may have upset her father. Jenny seems attracted to my criminal past and the stupid things I do. I don't care. I am more focused on having a girl being so affectionate with me. I learn that Jenny has an older sister who is away at college. She asks that I not ask about siblings. I eventually learn that her little brother died in a fire a few years ago and her parents are still upset about it.

After eating and spending some more time with Jenny and her parents, her father offers to drive me home. I try to explain how another train going the other way should arrive any minute. Jenny's father insists on driving me home.

When we arrive at my house, Jenny walks with me up to my house and her father watches from their car.

"He's going to show me his house really quickly," she yells at her father.

"Okay, but don't take too long," he responds.

Jenny whispers in my ear, "Let's go to the back of the house so my father can't see us."

When we get there, my kissing lessons are in full swing. I'm also encouraged to touch different parts of her body. Suddenly, she breaks free, tells me she has to go, and quickly walks to the front of the house. Jenny then gets in the car with her father and they leave.

I write some more stories that night. They now involve women, passion, kissing, and more. I realize I've changed once again. The world now looks like a very different place to me. I can see it in the stories I'm writing.

CHAPTER 14

A Ball of Confusion

Jenny and I talk daily on the phone. I talk my friend Neil about how I rode the train to see Jenny. He struggles to stop laughing at me. Neil suggests I try not to upset her father and ride my bike to Jenny's house. I think that hopping the train is quicker and easier, but riding my bike may make Jenny's father not look at me with that shocked expression. I start putting miles on my bike traveling to Jenny's house.

I have money from my criminal days. Her parents drive us to the movies. We go to eat at fast food restaurants, ice cream places, and I buy her little gifts. She shows me her appreciation in the most wonderful ways. I think this is the best time of my life.

I break down and introduce Jenny to my father and mother. My father smiles and is very nice about it. My mother looks at Jenny, then looks at me. She says that she can't believe it. I tried to warn Jenny about my mother before the introduction. After meeting my parents, Jenny looks at me with a confused expression. I tell her I understand—my parents are strange. She never asks about them again. I feel so confident in Jenny's feelings for me, I confess everything about my criminal past. It doesn't seem to bother her. She seems kind of excited by it. This feels strange to me, but I ignore it.

My neighbors look at me and Jenny through their windows. When they're on their front porch as we walk down the residential street, they wave at us. Jenny notices this and suggests we give them a show. She has her arm around my waist, kisses me on the cheek, and puts her head on my shoulder. Jenny then waves at the neighbor. She loves the looks we're getting. I think I'm enjoying them even more.

One time we're in a drug store and Jenny shows me some items I need to get, so we can make our relationship more adult. I have never heard of condoms before. She explains what they are and how they're used. I'm so embarrassed. I can't speak. Jenny tells me I don't have to get them today, but the sooner the better. Her older sister explained all about them to her. She can't wait until we can have sex. I'm feeling weird, but I know I like the idea.

The thought of buying condoms in a store causes me serious anxiety. I have the money, but I'm just too embarrassed. I resort to shoplifting and steal a box. This is horrible, but I keep telling myself there was no other way. I hide them in a place down by the river. If my parents ever find them, it will be horrible.

A few days after the drug store suggestion, I get a call from Jenny. She is going to be alone at her parents' house for a few hours. Her parents are driving to her sister's college for a visit. She explains how I have to be really sneaky because her nosy neighbors see everything. I have to ride my bike there, park it in the woods. I then have to be careful to not open the back fence door as it squeaks. This means I have to climb over the fence and go between the shed and her house. I then have to knock on her basement door. I feel like I'm a secret agent having a clandestine meeting with a spy associate.

I do exactly as she says, and I knock on the basement door. There is no answer and I knock again. I then think about going to the side of the house. I'm standing there feeling very nervous and yet excited. Suddenly, the basement door opens. Jenny is standing there in a bathrobe.

"Why are you wearing a bathrobe?" I ask.

"Why do you think? Get in here," she responds.

She takes my hand and leads me to an upstairs bathroom where a shower is running. Jenny verifies I have the condoms.

I'm confused and say, "If you want me to wait until you're done showering, that's okay."

Jenny smiles and says, "Oh, you really are new to this, aren't you?"

Her robe falls to the floor and reveals her beautiful young naked female body. The fear gives way to excitement as I struggle to remain calm. The afternoon is spent with Jenny teaching me about how adults have relationships. I'm a very dedicated student.

The world looks different after that day. I begin to grasp the reality of what people must do to create other people. I look at my parents and older people and refuse to think about them doing what is necessary to create children. The idea of those old people doing such a thing is pretty disgusting to me. All parents now look different to me.

My lessons about male and female relationships continue with Jenny. She's an excellent teacher. It is something we do by the river, in the woods, behind her home, in her bedroom, and once in the basement of her grandmother's house. Anyplace where it seems we can get away with it is a place where we try. I discover my male hormones' power over me. More power than anything else I have ever experienced before in my life.

Jenny begins to be busy with other things. The time we spend together slowly decreases. She spends days with her older sister, doing things with her parents, and visiting relatives. When I'm not with Jenny, I spend time writing stories and being with Roger or Neil.

My introduction to drinking occurs with Roger. He finds two six packs of beer hidden in bushes near his house. Roger calls me and says to get over to his house right away. There is nobody there except us and the beer. We drink the beer, and I experience being drunk, bed spins, and depositing the contents of my stomach into the toilet because of alcohol for the first time. There starts to be more alcohol at Roger's house since his brother Simon is back from college. At Roger's house, his middle brother Nate routinely offers me beer or shots of whiskey. I initially declined his offers, but now I accept them.

Nate comes up to me one day when I'm at their house. He starts asking about Jenny.

He says, "You know that girl's odometer has more miles on it than a thirty-year-old city bus, right?"

I laugh but have no idea what he's talking about.

"What's an odometer?" I ask.

Nate laughs as he thinks I'm just playing stupid. I don't want to tell him I'm not playing, so I let it go. Drinking at Roger's place becomes a regular thing. One time Simon asks me to put some money toward a bottle of wine. I give him twenty dollars. He smiles and says that will do just fine.

After not hearing from Jenny for a few days, I get a call from her. She asks me if I know about the party going on at Roger's house in a few days. I tell her I'm helping them plan it and set it up. She says this is good, and she will be there. We talk a long time, and I feel good when the phone conversation ends. I just get anxious when I realize I have to make another trip to the drug store.

On the day of the party, the inside and outside of Roger's home have kids my age and older walking around drinking beer and smoking joints. There is loud music being played and the sound of people talking is all around. I see Jenny, walk up to her, try to kiss her, and she turns her head.

"What's wrong?" I ask.

She looks around and then whispers in my ear, "Friends of my older sister are here, and they will report everything I do to my parents."

"You're holding an open can of beer," I say.

Jenny smiles and motions for me to follow her. We go to an abandoned small trailer on the edge of the property. Jenny looks around and then quickly opens the door and pushes me inside. After finishing our beers, Jenny gets undressed, and we have at it for a while. We get our clothes on and are sitting at a table in the kitchen holding hands.

"I've missed you, but I need a favor from you," says Jenny.

"Oh, what do you need?" I respond.

"I have an old boyfriend who stole my grandmother's bracelet. I want you to get it back from him."

"How?"

"It's easy, you just go to his house when I tell you. His bedroom window is always open. You just need to climb up a tree, get onto the porch roof of his house, go into his bedroom, go into the top drawer of his dresser, get the bracelet, and bring it back to me. Won't that be easy?"

"I don't know. Sounds like something a guy my age could get sent to juvenile hall for doing. That is a place I don't want to visit again during my life."

Jenny begins to plead, saying, "Oh, come on, it's just one little thing I'm asking you to do. Let's face it, you're a thief, what difference does it make to you? Why would you care? You've already been to juvenile hall once. What difference does it make if you go again?"

I can't believe what she has just said to me.

"I don't want to get in trouble again. I'm done doing that stuff."

"Then why did you steal the condoms?"

"That's different. I was too embarrassed to buy them."

I think Jenny can tell she's hurt my feelings. I'm struggling to look at her. She gets close, puts her arm around me, and starts touching my hair.

"I'm sorry, but my grandmother's bracelet means so much to me. It seems like something that would be easy for you to do."

"If it's so easy, why don't you do it?"

This makes Jenny furious. I've never seen her this angry.

Jenny screams, "I'm not a thief, I thought I meant something to you. All I ask is for you to do one little thing for me like get back my grandmother's bracelet and you won't do it. I don't want to see you anymore."

When Jenny leaves, the door to the trailer is slammed shut by her so hard the entire structure shakes. I hear a knock at the door. Roger comes in and asks what's wrong. I just tell him Jenny and I just had a fight. Roger explains that his older brother Simon and his girlfriend have been waiting to use the trailer if I'm done with it.

I spend the rest of the party with Jenny ignoring me and talking with other guys. When she sees me look at her, she puts her arm around the guy she is talking with at the time. I'm having a miserable time and leave the party early. As I'm walking out, Jenny gets my attention. I turn around to see her with her arm around another guy.

She looks at me and says, "Oh, and please don't forget to not call me."

Jenny and the guy she's with begin laughing.

The next few days are a struggle for me. Part of me wants to take my bike, go into her old boyfriend's house, and get the bracelet. She and I would be back together, and I'd never do anything like that again. The other part of me believes doing such a thing would be crazy. I just don't want to take a chance on getting arrested again. I feel awful about stealing the condoms. If I get Jenny back her grandmother's bracelet, I wonder what else she will ask her thief boyfriend to do for her. I hate thinking about it.

Days come and go with me just exploring the river and writing my stories in the evening. I watch television with my mother and have no idea what she is saying to me most of the time. I don't care. Having parents who ignore me most of the time has become a blessing.

It's been almost two weeks since I spoke with Roger. He calls me up and tells me about a party happening in another town. His brother will drive us there. They're going to leave their house around midnight and asks me to meet them there. I tell him I'll see him at midnight.

I always assume too many things. When Roger contacted me, I assumed I'd go down there at midnight, we'd get into a car, and drive to a party. This does not happen. I get there around midnight. Their house has no lights on inside. I go onto the porch and Roger is standing there. He whispers to me to be quiet and follow him.

It seems that their father didn't like the idea of his son using the family car to go to a party in the middle of the night. Roger now tells me it is necessary to commandeer their mother's car since his father's car is in the garage.

Roger's brother Nate gets in the car, puts it in gear, and lets it coast down the driveway. Once it is there, Roger and I start pushing the car toward the end of the block. They don't want to take any chances waking up their parents, so they don't want to start the car until it has been pushed a few blocks away. It's dark except for a few street lights and outside lights on some lawns. The only sounds are crickets, owls, and the rumble of trucks on a distant highway.

We get three blocks from Roger's home. When we get in, Nate starts the car, and we're on our way.

Nate looks at me and says, "Don't worry, I have a driver's license."

Roger says, "Yeah, dad said it's a junior driver's license and you shouldn't be driving after midnight."

"Do you want to walk?" yells Nate.

In a meek voice, Roger says, "No."

During the drive to the party, I experience other types of sibling rivalry that are common in most homes. Nate threatens Roger with walking home after the party if he gets on his nerves. Roger threatens Nate with telling their mom what they've done. Nate is calling Roger names he doesn't like, and Roger is telling his brother to shut up. It is obvious to me their relationship is not one of ignoring one another like me and my half-sister. I'm really glad when we get to the party. I think about walking home when it's over.

CHAPTER 15

True Colors

I'm four years old and sitting in a sandbox in my backyard. It rained the night before and the sand is moist. I have on my favorite coat and tennis shoes. My mother led me out here and then disappeared back into the house. It's quiet, and I can't see anybody else in any of the nearby yards. I stick my shovel in the sand for something to do.

I notice a neighborhood dog come to the gate in the backyard. His name is Duke, and I think he is the nicest dog I've ever met. He barks at me and then runs to the woods and comes back. He then barks at me again. Duke wants me to follow him.

I get out of my sandbox and open the gate. I then follow Duke. He takes me to a spot in the woods where there is a picnic bench. I'm talking to Duke the entire time, and he seems to understand me. I get sticks, leaves, and some pine cones and I'm building something as I sit at the picnic bench. I hear twigs snapping and footsteps. Duke is up and growling. I ask him what's wrong, but Duke is focused in the direction of the sound. The footsteps stop. I can't see anything. Duke walks toward the sound growling. I then hear him barking. The footsteps get fainter as something is running away. When he comes back, I pet Duke and tell him I love him.

After a while, Duke barks for me to follow him. I get off the picnic bench and Duke leads me back to my yard. He wants me to go back to my sandbox. I thank Duke for a great time. I go into my yard, close the gate, and hear my mother calling for me to come inside.

Duke was my first friend that I can remember. I knew he would protect me against anything that would try to harm me. I loved Duke with all the innocence and sincerity a four-year-old child has within them.

When we get to the party, it is at a house that sits away from the other nearby houses. There is quite a bit of lawn and woods surrounding it. Several cars are parked everywhere. Just like at the party that took place at Roger and Nate's house, there are kids my age or older walking around holding plastic cups, as well as cans of beer. Loud music is being played. There is a children's plastic pool in the middle of the back lawn. It is occupied by various people in different stages of undress. The loud music is blended with talking and laughter.

As I walk around, I see Roger and Nate have found their girlfriends and wave to me. I see some other people I know. There is Tanya's boyfriend Jack. I say hello and he says hello back to me. I go to where there is a huge container of ice with beer and get one. Drinking is not something that appeals to me. I hope having a few beers will change how I'm feeling about things right now.

I talk to a few people. Someone asks if I know how to play an instrument or can sing because they're getting a band together. I'm honest and say I have no musical talent. Those guys move on in their quest for a musician to complete their band. I keep walking and enjoying the music.

I hear from behind me someone say, "Hey, Bill Shakespeare, it's the Bill Shakespeare guy."

I turn around and two guys I don't know walk up to me. One is about my age, and I recognize him as Ralph from class. I don't know the other guy who is a bit bigger. Ralph tells me this is his older brother.

Ralph points to me and says to his brother, "This is the guy who talked about calling William Shakespeare Bill. It was the funniest thing I've ever seen in class. Mrs. Nardonner didn't know what to do, it was great."

The older brother looks at me and says, "Good one."

I talk to them a bit and soon realize they're both real drunk. According to Ralph, I'm a bit of a legend in school. Even other teachers talk about the Bill Shakespeare kid. It feels good being told I made so many people laugh. I didn't get a good grade, but at least I made some kids laugh.

Somebody calls to Ralph and his brother from down the lawn. When the two of them realize who it is, they tell me they want to talk to this person and walk away. I wonder if they'll be sober enough to even stand up later.

The worst possible thing then happens to me. It occurs in less than a second. I see Jenny hanging on another guy. She has a beer in her hand and is part of a large group that is just standing together talking. Jenny doesn't recognize me, so I just get away from that area as quickly as possible. I don't want to talk to her. I wish I hadn't seen her. I am extremely upset. I'm thinking about leaving and walking the long distance back to my house.

From behind me, I hear Jenny say, "Are you just going to run away from me?"

I quickly turn around and face her and say, "Look, you're here with other guys. I'm not going to bother you. So, you just leave me alone, and I stay away from you. Okay?"

Anger shows on Jenny's face as she says, "So, that's it, huh? You have all kinds of sex with me and then just leave. It was all about sex with you, wasn't it?"

"You're the one who broke up with me."

"Because you're an asshole. You'll steal for everyone else but not for me."

"What are you talking about?"

"You couldn't get my grandmother's bracelet but if we're going to have sex then stealing condoms is just great. Where was your fear of juvenile hall when you were stealing condoms? Huh?"

"You said it would be so easy to get your grandmother's bracelet. Why didn't you get it back from your old boyfriend yourself?"

"For your information, I did. I had to get back with him, but I have the bracelet, no thanks to you."

"So, what's the problem?"

Jenny lets out an angry groan and says, "You used me for sex and then got rid of me, that's the problem."

I yell, "You're the one who got rid of me. You're crazy."

I turn and walk away then hear Jenny yell, "I understand why your mother doesn't like you. It's not easy to like an asshole like you."

I stop with my back toward Jenny. I am so hurt and angry about what she has just said to me. I clench my fists and take some deep breaths. I tell myself I don't have to ever see her again. I continue walking and I hear her behind me laughing.

I keep walking and hear her yell, "You're pathetic."

After the incident with Jenny, I go to where the albums are being played and start looking at the music. I have another beer, talk to some more people, and don't see Jenny around. I'm hoping she and her boyfriend have left.

I go to explore the woods and see couples doing what teenage couples do in the woods. I decide it may be a good idea to let them have their privacy. I don't miss Jenny, but I miss having a girlfriend. I look around at the girls at the party and exchange glances with a few of them. I'm working up the nerve to approach one of them when I hear off to the side.

"That's him, but don't hurt him."

It's Jenny with a guy who is walking toward me and seems pretty angry. I don't know how old he is, but this guy has a full beard and is a little taller than me. He walks up to me and pushes me.

The guy says, "So, you're the asshole who used Jenny for sex and dumped her?"

I push him back and say, "You got it all wrong. She's a liar, she broke up with me."

I don't want to fight this guy. I've not been in a fight for a long time. I don't want this to happen. The guy grabs me and whispers, "I hate assholes like you. Did you hit her when she refused sex? Did you do that to her?"

I break free from the guy. Now people are gathered around, holding their beers and plastic cups as if they're at a sporting event.

I yell, "You don't get it. She is out of her mind."

The guy tries to hit me. I'm lucky—he's very drunk so avoiding his punch is pretty easy. I then have a clear shot and I hit him in his stomach as hard as I can. He goes down and groans for a few seconds. I resist the temptation to get on him and start punching his face. The desire to kick him in the head is so strong. I'm hoping he gives up.

I hear Jenny yell, "Leave him alone and stop punching him, asshole."

The guy gets up, and we both have our fists ready to fight. I give into my anger, and I'm ready for a fight. The next thing I see is the back of a girl's head. She's yelling at Jenny's boyfriend as well as Jenny. This girl is telling them off and is angry. I lower my fists and just stand there. Jenny and her boyfriend turn and slowly walk away. When the girl turns around, I see a beautiful female with red hair, freckles, and a friendly smile. It's Tanya.

Tanya takes my hand, leads me away, and says, "We have to talk right now."

We go to the end of the property where the cars are parked. She opens up a car door and tells me to get inside. Once inside the car, Tanya looks at me and smiles.

"I didn't think I'd see you again like this. The guy you punched will be eighteen in a few months. Nobody else would have ever dared hit him," she says.

"Well, he is pretty drunk, and he started it," I respond.

Tanya goes on to tell me she knows this guy from school. He has friends and an older brother at the party. None of them are going to accept me punching him in front of everybody. She says I need to leave or I'm going to get beat up by that group of guys. I tell her I have to let my friends know I'm leaving. Tanya says she'll take care of it. I describe my friends and she knows their girlfriends. She quickly gets out of the car.

When she's gone, I look around and things are hanging from the rear view mirror forming Tanya's name. There are foam dice that she must have won at an amusement park. In the back seat are magazines. They are copies of *Seventeen*, *Tiger Beat*, and a copy of *Vogue*. I'm disappointed when I don't see any baseball magazines.

The car is pretty new and very clean. I open the glove box and there is makeup in there. I close it and then just settle down and wait for Tanya's return. After about fifteen minutes, the driver-side door opens. Tanya gets in and informs me she told my friend Roger I'll be leaving with her. I look through the windshield and the guy I punched sees me. He whistles and a group of guys starts coming in the direction of Tanya's car. When he points to me in the car, they begin coming straight toward us.

Tanya quickly starts the car, puts it in gear, heads toward the road, and says, "Not a moment too soon."

As we're going down the road, Tanya tells me she has her driver's license now and her parents got her a car. I hear how she knows the guy I punched because his family lives near her. She has known him since kindergarten. I am informed he is not a bad guy but will believe anything a female who he's dating tells him. Tanya talks about colleges she is thinking about attending after high school.

When she stops talking, I say, "Why did you save me tonight?"

Tanya puts her hand on my shoulder for a second before slowly removing it.

"Because you're my friend. I like you. You are a very nice guy. I don't want anything bad to happen to you."

"I wish you were my girlfriend instead of Jenny, but you have Jack."

Tanya laughs.

"Jack and I broke up. He has a new girlfriend. It worked out okay because I have a new boyfriend."

"When you break up with someone, let the rest of us guys know and give us a chance."

Tanya laughs again. She asks if I dated Jenny. I tell her yes, and Tanya seems angry. She tells me Jenny is really messed up. Her older sister is a fantastic student and has even better looks than Jenny. Their youngest was a little boy who died in a house fire. Rumor has it that Jenny's parents blame her because of something she may have done to cause the fire. Jenny is too young to remember anything. People who know her family say Jenny's parents are resentful toward her. She has been boy crazy for a while. Jenny is an angry person. She is a good student, but nothing like her older sister. Her parents constantly talk about her older sister's success in school. Jenny always experiences the resentment of her parents for what happened to her younger brother. I'm sure it's difficult for her.

When we get to my house, Tanya and I just sit and talk some more. She is the first person I ever tell about my stories. Tanya seems excited and wants to know more about them. She tells me she'd love to read my stories if I am okay with it. I tell Tanya I'll think about it.

Before I get out of the car, Tanya gives me a short hug and tells me to be careful. The guys I almost tangled with at the party are pretty crazy. I look at Tanya and my feelings for her are stronger than I realized. I almost tell her I love her. She drives away, and I stand there saying how much I love her to myself.

CHAPTER 16

A New Leaf With Old Problems

I spend the next several days after the party in my bedroom writing stories. My parents seem to take notice. When I tell them what I'm doing, my mother tells me I should be outside doing something because it is summer. My father looks at me, and I can see in his eyes that he knows this is important to me.

I walk onto the front porch one evening after being over at a friend's house. My father is there reading the newspaper. When he sees me, he points to the chair next to him and asks me to sit down.

"What's going on?" I say.

My father rubs his chin, which is his habit before saying something he's been thinking about.

"You know, I looked at typewriters for you. The only ones in stores now are those electric ones. They're a bit too expensive."

I'm touched that my father remembered and looked into getting me one.

"That's okay. I understand," I say.

Then his eyes light up.

"At the hospital, they bought everyone in the office a new electric typewriter. I asked what they were doing with their old manual typewriters. I was told they were just going to put them in storage. I talked to the guy who is the head of administration and asked him if I could have one of those manual typewriters. I told him how you wanted one because you write stories. Guess what?"

I start getting excited.

"What?"

"He gave me one of their newer ones, some ribbons, and paper for you. I thanked him and told him this would probably make you really happy."

"Where is it?"

"I put it upstairs on the desk in your bedroom. I hope you like it."

For the first time in my life, I feel like hugging my dad.

"Thank you so much."

I try to hug my dad, and it is a very awkward moment. Neither of us is comfortable with it. I then go up to my bedroom.

Sitting on my desk is an Underwood manual typewriter with a plastic cover. It's similar to the one I used during school when I took a typing class. I slowly remove the plastic cover. I look it over and the typewriter seems to be in great condition. On the one side of the typewriter are two reams of office paper. On the other side are at least six new ribbons. I can't control my excitement and don't know what to do first. I put on some music and just stare at it for a few special moments. Visions of all my favorite writers from John Steinbeck to George Orwell, Agatha Christie, Norman Mailer, and others sitting down at a typewriter to create their stories goes through my mind. It's now possible for me to do the same thing with my typewriter. I feel a special connection with all of those writers.

It's getting toward the end of summer. School will start soon. I'm ready for the new school year. I know I'm much different from the guy I was at the beginning of summer. For the first time in my life, I am looking forward to school. Much of my time now consists of writing stories. I don't have the courage to send any of them out to a publisher, but I am seeing a few that I might consider sending.

When Tommy was around, he showed me a large creek located on the edge of town. Lots of people go to different places along the creek to swim. There are fires started and parties take place at various locations. You never know who you're going to come across at the creek.

I've worked hard to forget the pains from the past. Not letting my anger take me is getting easier and easier. I've not been in trouble or had a fight for a long time. My parents are now in a routine. My mother takes care of the home and is in regular contact with my half-sister and the children from her previous marriage. My father goes to work, comes home, reads his newspaper on the porch, then goes to his bedroom to watch television. The anger and bitterness of the past are always just below the surface with all of us. We don't talk about things from the past. My parents have become good at not arguing. They now occasionally go out to dinner with one another. Things are different.

I soon learn the past is something many people hold onto and look through to see what is around them. Anger and resentment about things that have happened fuel their behavior. No matter how much anyone lets go of the past, others hold onto it too tightly in the present. This is my biggest struggle with people right now.

I'm walking down by the creek on a summer evening. There doesn't seem to be anybody around. It's peaceful just listening to the water rushing over rocks as it makes its way downstream. I hear voices and wait to see who is approaching. It's two guys who are bigger than me with a kid I recognize named Stan. The other bigger guy is the son of the policeman who held me down as my mother's boyfriend hit me.

When I had the fight with my mother's boyfriend, I didn't realize he had a son named Stan who is my age. Stan tried to pick a fight with me in school, but he's much smaller than I am. I simply picked him up and put him headfirst into a tall garbage bin. Other kids were laughing as they saw two legs sticking up out of the garbage bin moving back and forth. This was accompanied by the muffled sounds of obscenities from a rather upset student.

The other kids around me were laughing so hard, we couldn't pull him out of the garbage bin. When he did get out, there was everything from pencil shavings to bits of old art projects on his head and body. Then we really laughed. When he pointed to me and kept swearing, I just laughed and pointed at all the stuff on his head and shirt. He told a teacher. I admitted to what I had done and got hit with a paddle and a suspension, but I felt it was worth it. I only wish I could have been there when he told his father what happened and who did it to him.

When the three of them see me, I don't run. I stand my ground. I don't want a fight; I don't want anything to happen. Stan starts yelling at me. I want to tell Stan I'm sorry for what I did and explain how he gave me no choice by trying to pick a fight with me.

When they see me, I hear Stan yell, "That's the piece of shit that got into a fight with my dad and stuck me in a garbage can."

They all come over and surround me in seconds.

I say to Stan, "Look, I'm sorry for the garbage can thing, but you shouldn't have tried to pick a fight with me. I got paddled and suspended. What more do you want?"

The policeman's son hits me in the head and says, "You shouldn't have tried to beat up his old man. Are you an animal who was never taught any manners?"

I push him hard and it throws him off balance.

I yell, "That happened a long time ago. What's the matter with you? You have nothing else to do but think about me and Stan's dad in a brawl?"

Stan says, "Hey, I have an idea, let's duct tape his hands and feet together and throw him in the creek. I'll give you guys each ten bucks to do it."

I try to laugh it off when Stan pulls money from his pockets. One of the bigger guys is behind me before I realize it. When Stan finishes speaking, the guy grabs me from behind. I try to get free, but he is just too strong.

The policeman's son takes out duct tape from his pocket. He and Stan are able to tape my feet together no matter how hard I struggle. He says, "We can use this now and buy more tape later to fix the car."

I keep struggling as much as I can, but they're just too strong. They manage to get my hands taped. During the entire time duct tape is being put on me, Stan is laughing, hitting me in the face, and kicking me.

"You better know how to swim, asshole, or you gonna die," says the policeman's son.

As I struggle, the two big guys pick me up, take me to the edge of the creek and throw me up into the air and I go toward the middle of the creek. I see a rock coming toward my head and turn to avoid it. I feel myself hitting the water with a loud splash. After going underwater for a few seconds, I come to the top and get a breath of air. I can hear Stan and the others laughing at the edge of the creek. The current of the creek takes me downstream.

With my hands and feet taped together, I can still do a doggy paddle move in the water. I slowly make it to the bank. It takes me a while, but I get the tape off of my wrists and then feet. I now feel something I haven't experienced in a long time. It's a calm rage. I don't feel like yelling or screaming. Something has taken me over as I make my way to Stan's house.

I wait between two houses across the street from Stan's house for over an hour. I'm still pretty wet. My tennis shoes are soaked, my hair has bits of sand and debris in it, and I smell like creek water. None of that matters; I am solely focused on Stan.

Finally, I see Stan walking down the street. I come out between the houses, cross the road, and walk toward him.

Stan starts laughing when he sees me and says, "Hey asshole, I'm sorry about the creek thing, but you shouldn't have just stood there when you saw us."

I say, "You tried to kill me."

Stan is shocked when I walk right up to him and punch him in the face. His mouth is bloody. He falls but quickly stands up and pushes me. I go back a few steps and then just calmly walk toward me again.

"You want those guys I was with to come and beat you up?"

"Maybe I'll pay them thirty dollars to tape you up and throw you in the creek. They do have their price, don't they?"

Stan charges me. I feel no pain from him hitting me and kicking me in the side. I grab him, turn around as I'm holding him, and then let go. Stan goes into the air and then hits the sidewalk hard. I then calmly again start walking toward him. When he looks at me, I can tell that Stan is terrified right now. My anger has completely taken me over.

Stan tries to run and I run after him. He goes onto the porch of his house, through the front door screaming to his mother that someone is trying to kill him. Stan goes up the stairs of his house. His mother comes out and tries to stop me from going up the stairs. I push her out of the way and continue up the steps. She threatens to call the police, and I don't care.

When Stan goes into his bedroom, he tries to close the door, but I'm too strong for him and force my way inside. His mouth is bloody, but I get him, wrestle him down and start hitting him in the face. Stan grabs a hockey stick lying near his bed and hits me in the head with it. I'm stunned and fall back. When I see Stan run out of the room, I'm after him.

Stan goes out of his house and runs down the street with me behind him. He goes across the park, the highway, and down to the railroad tracks. I'm still after him. There is a stopped train on the track. Stan climbs over it, and I climb over it. He tries to hide in the woods, but I find him. Stan then makes his way back over the stopped train and up to the town's sidewalks. I'm still after him. I'm running toward him when he goes into a church. I'm about to go into the church when I hear a loudspeaker from a car.

"Stop it now and come down here."

When I turn around, it's one of the local policemen. I've never seen him before. He must be new. The policeman tells me to get in the car. I hesitate because reality comes crashing down on me. I realize I just did some pretty bad things.

On the way to the police station, I tell the new police officer what happened to me at the creek. He seems surprised. I don't think he believes me at first, but I do smell like creek water and look like someone who has been in the creek. I get to the police station, and I'm put in a room by myself. Time seems to be passing slowly.

The regrets start to come into my mind. I regret not running when I saw those guys. I regret even going to the creek today. The biggest regret I have is not being able once again to control my temper. I hate how I look and especially how I smell.

After about an hour, the new policeman comes and gets me. I'm taken to the office of the chief of police. In there is Stan, the policeman's son, and his father all sitting at a table. I sit down across from them. The chief of police is at the head of the table and asks Stan what happened. According to Stan, they saw me, and I asked them to tie me up and throw me in the creek because I wanted to see if I could get free.

"If that's true, why did you pay the other two guys ten bucks to tie me up and throw me in the creek?"

The policeman looks at his son and asks if that's true.

His son says, "Aw, come on now. Dad, it was a joke is all. He shouldn't have gotten all upset and beat up Stan. So, what if Stan paid us some money? He owes us money for lots of things. It was no big deal until the jackass over there made it one. He's the one who needs to go to jail. I have no idea why Stan and I are here."

There is silence. The chief of police takes off his glasses and rubs his face and lets out a breath.

"Let me see if I understand what happened. Stan and his two older friends come across someone near the creek. They never said he did anything to provoke them. They tape his hands and feet together and throw him in the creek after Stan pays them each ten dollars."

"He asked us to do it," says Stan.

"If I asked you to do it, why did you pay them? Why would I come to kick your ass, you idiot?"

Stan points to me and yells, "He pushed my mother in my house."

The chief of police tells everyone to be quiet. I'm told to go back to the room where I had been, and I gladly go there.

It seems like a long time before the new police officer comes into the room. He sits down next to me and looks at some papers he's holding.

"Today is your lucky day. Stan's mother isn't going to press charges against you for assault as well as breaking and entering her home," he says.

I respond very slowly and say, "So what happens to Stan and those other guys? They taped my hands and feet together and then threw me into a creek. Stan paid them to do it. If I didn't know how to swim, I could have died."

"Well, sometimes pranks get out of hand. I don't think they meant to harm you. They probably just wanted to scare you. They made some dumb decisions. There were only four people at that creek today. We talked with the other guy on the phone about it. He says you were running your mouth at them. Three of the people at the creek say you were the problem. I think you should walk out of the police station today and be thankful you're not being charged with any crimes."

I'm angry, really angry. I don't know what to say. I know this isn't right, but I also don't know what to do about it. I decide to drop it. I go home. When my parents ask me what happened, I just tell them I fell in the creek.

I think about the fear I had of Derrick laughing when we had a fight a few months ago. Why he didn't stop now makes sense. He couldn't control himself and wouldn't stop. I understand what Derrick was feeling, and it scares me. The lies Stan and his friends told are much easier for people to understand than telling the truth. This is a lesson I learned early about surviving in this world. It's also a belief I have that is only reinforced by experience.

CHAPTER 17

Weaponized Truth

School starts and I'm glad to be back in a routine. After my last encounter with the law, I spend much of my time alone in my house. Going to school daily, I regularly see other kids. My new approach to school is to try to be a good student. I'm determined to do well this year. I keep telling myself no more fighting or getting suspended. I tell myself I won't ever get in trouble with the law again. This is what I repeat over and over in my mind.

Eventually, all of my stories are typed and put in folders. It was a lot of work and took me a significant amount of time, but I get all of my stories typed. I even subscribe to a writing magazine Neil had given me. I have a lot of things going on with writing except self-confidence. I regularly look at my stories and don't know which one I should send out, or if I should send any of them. I go back and forth and then just put them away. I struggle with my previous poor grades and a feeling that I'm a criminal. Every time I think about sending out a story, I quickly talk myself out of it. It's a constant frustration.

I notice some girls at school. I make quite a few friends who are girls, but I have no desire to get too close to any of them. My Jenny experience is not completely out of my mind. I think Neil is taking every advanced course offered by the school this year. He and his girlfriend broke up. I ask him what happened, and he tells me they got tired of one another. I admire his ability to do school work.

I've learned to not ask Neil too many questions about things that interest him. One weekend he tells me he's thinking of becoming an entomologist. I don't know what he's talking about. Neil then tells me that's the study of insects. I ask him why he wants to study bugs. The next thing I know I'm being given books, magazines, and told all sorts of stories about fascinating insect species. I like going to see Neil, but I was glad to get out of his house that day.

I begin to wonder if people like me can change. Is it possible for someone to turn away from their true self? Can a person actually overcome things inside themselves they can't control? I want to be good like some other kids in school. It's a struggle for me. I see too much bullying happening. When I walk away from it, I feel ashamed I didn't help the kid getting bullied. The first time was tough, the second time I almost broke. The third time, I can no longer take it. I just want to avoid getting into trouble so much.

The school is now divided into three separate and distinct groups. Kids in the advanced shop classes are referred to as the greasers. The kids in sports are known as the jocks. The good students are known as the nerds. Then there is the rest of us. Those who don't fit specifically into any group. I'm not a greaser, jock, or nerd. I'm a wandering student nomad who slips between the cracks of social classification.

There is a guy who helps me with my math homework and is always nice to me. His name is Victor. He is a smart kid and has helped me and some other kids with math. Victor has black bushy hair and glasses that seem too big. He's constantly pushing them up his nose. He explains that he sniffles a lot because he has allergies.

We are in the boy's room washing our hands and talking. Victor's father is a manager at a plant that bottles pickles. He tells me how he is so tired of eating pickles and that even hearing the word gherkin makes him want to scream. I laugh.

The door opens and some greaser kids walk in. They all have on jean jackets and smell like cigarette smoke. They all instantly take out cigarettes and light them up.

When we try to leave, one of them grabs Victor and says, "Hey pickle boy, you got any money? I'm broke."

Victor responds in his nasally voice, "Leave me alone, I don't have any money today."

I focus on Victor saying today as if it's happened before. I have a feeling he's previously given these greasers money. I'm truly struggling. I could leave now and leave Victor in the clutches of the greasers. Nobody would think less of me. I would avoid any trouble. Something inside me breaks. I throw my books down and go over to the greaser holding Victor and push his hand away.

"Leave him alone, he's done nothing to you."

The greaser looks at his friend and smiles.

"Or you're going to do what? In case you don't realize it, there are three of us and only one of you. So, why don't you leave?"

My rage takes me. In an instant, I grab the greaser guy before he knows what has happened, and I have him up against the wall. His unlit cigarette goes in the air. I start pushing my forearm into his throat so it hurts.

I yell, "Anybody comes near me and I'll break his Adam's apple."

The greaser kid in my grasp motions for his friends to back away.

I then get close to his face and say in a low voice, "I'm not a smart kid, or a greaser, or a jock. I have nothing to lose. I don't care if I get suspended or even arrested. It's happened before. I'm considered crazy. But if you bother Victor again and I find out, I will hurt you."

The greaser is struggling to speak but says, "Is that so? If you don't let go of me right now, you are the one who is going to get hurt."

"Have it your way."

I start to squeeze a little harder and the greaser struggles more. His friends begin to come toward me.

The door suddenly opens up. A teacher comes in and says, "What's going on here? The bell rang five minutes ago."

I let the greaser go. He straightens his jacket and runs his hands through his hair. I then say, "We were just talking."

The teacher motions for us to get out of the bathroom.

A few days later when I see Victor, he is upset with me. He says I didn't have to defend him. I ask Victor how long he's been giving money to those guys. He screams it's none of my business. I try to explain what those guys are doing to him is wrong. I ask Victor to tell me if any of those greaser kids bother him again. Victor tells me that it's his life, and he doesn't want my help. He can take care of himself.

I'm confused by his response. I thought protecting someone against a bully would be a good thing. Victor stops helping me with math. He treats me as if I've done something horrible to him. I don't understand and feel very confused. The world makes absolutely no sense to me.

In the fall, I'm at Roger's house. He and Nate have decided to form a band. They ask me to join them. I'm honest and tell them the tragic tale of my short-lived guitar lesson experience. Nate asks me how many chords I can play on the guitar. I count them in my head and say about eight. Nate says that's perfect. Roger is going to play the drums. His only experience is trying to follow along when listening to the radio. Nate tells me I can play my chords on an old electric guitar Roger's family has in their garage. A friend is going to play bass guitar and Nate will sing.

The first day we try to practice doesn't go well. One of the strings is missing from the electric guitar and the amplifier doesn't work right. The kid who is the bass player fixes the guitar, and Nate fixes the amplifier. Things go a little better after that and our playing improves.

For about two weeks, we meet in the garage at Roger's house and practice. We master about four songs and there are a few others we come close to playing so people will recognize them. Nate believes we're ready for a concert.

It's a rather cool Saturday in autumn when we set up outside the house of the bass player. I look around and tell Nate nobody is here, and he tells me not to worry. Calls are being made. In a short time, a group of kids shows up near the garage to watch us play.

We start playing and things are going well. I have no idea what I'm doing but nobody seems to notice as I make it up. Roger tells me he is doing the same thing. Nate is wearing a crazy hat with a feather in it and bright blue shoes as he sings. During one of the songs, Nate introduces the rest of the band but makes up names for us. He calls the bass player Aurelius, refers to Roger as Josephus, and me as Maximilian. Nate tells the small crowd that his name is Lucian.

I lean back toward Roger and say, "What's with the names?"

Roger says, "Nate is taking his second year of Latin so everybody has a Latin name,"

"Oh."

During the middle of a song, Nate points to Roger for a drum solo, and he does great. Nate then points to the bass player for a solo, he also does great. Then he points to me for a guitar solo. I just do my best and I'm surprised I do okay. The bass player comes over, turns his back to the crowd, and tells me that it was good for someone who has no idea what he's doing.

All of us are having a great time. We're not aware the bass player's parents are getting calls about the noise. I don't realize some neighbors are screaming for us to knock it off. None of us notice the cars driving by and beeping at us as the drivers yell for us to stop it. We just play every song we know, and then play some others again. We are all lost in the world of music-making.

I have my eyes closed and I'm not aware of anything but playing music. Suddenly, I hear the bass player tell me to stop playing. I do this and look up to see a police car in the street right in front of the house. Two police officers get out and walk toward us. They both know me. I'm fighting my feelings of panic. I want to drop the guitar and start running. I just stand motionless.

I have always been amazed by how wild Nate and Roger seem, and yet they've never been in trouble with the police or even in school. I have a feeling I'm going to be taken to the police station. I take off the guitar and carefully put it on the ground.

When the police come close, Nate stands in front of them and yells, "What's the problem? A few kids make some music for the neighborhood and can't continue because a few idiot neighbors don't like it. If that's what you're going to tell me, that's bullshit."

One of the police officers looks past Nate and sees me. He elbows the other police officer and points to me. They roll their eyes and smile.

"You're making too much noise. You can't play here and form a crowd like this unless you have an entertainment permit. Do you have one?" asks one of the policemen.

Nate then starts to get real belligerent. He screams, "Screw that permit shit. This is a free country and if we want to make music, we're gonna make music. So why don't you just buzz off and go back to police piggy land, huh? Go harass old people for jaywalking. That's all you guys are good for anyway."

I run to Nate and get between him and the police. Nate starts struggling with me. I believe he wants to hit one of the police officers. Roger and the bass player also work with me to keep Nate away from the police.

The bass player says, "Sorry, he is just excited about playing in front of a crowd. We're all excited. We'll stop if that will make things better."

One of the policemen is the father of the guy who helped throw me into the creek. He gets close to Nate and says, "You don't want this trouble."

Nate yells, "Screw you, asshole."

The policeman then points to me and says, "Ask your friend here what happens when you get taken down to the police station. If you want to know what it's like to get arrested and go to juvenile hall, you just ask him. He's done all of it. Now I want you to stop making all this noise and if I have to come back, I'll arrest all of you. Do you understand?"

Nate, Roger, and the bass player look at me with expressions of shock. Learning about my past from the police has stunned them. I feel sick inside. I know they heard the rumors about me being a criminal. I admitted everything to Jenny, but not them. When they kidded me about being a bad boy, I just played it off and changed the subject. They didn't think of me as a criminal. I realize things will now change between me and them. I didn't lie to them, but I didn't trust them enough to be honest about my past.

"We'll do that and won't have any more problems," says Roger.

When the police officers walk away, Nate looks at me and says, "You've been arrested and sent to juvenile hall? I don't believe it."

I say, "Believe it, he told you the truth. I never said anything about it because I didn't want anyone to know. I'm sorry if it makes you hate me."

We start to put things in the back of Nate's car. We drive back to their place. It's with a heavy heart that I answer their questions about what I did and why I was arrested. I even tell them about being thrown in the creek. I don't share about getting into a fight with my mother's boyfriend and the policeman holding me down. Some things are too painful to share. None of them can believe it. They all thought I was just a nice kid. I feel horrible.

After we get back to Nate's house and unload everything, they ask if I want to stick around for a while. Roger says we could have some beer and listen to music. I tell them I just want to go home. I get on my bike, ride past my house, and then keep riding for a few hours before I come back. I'm better after the bike ride.

Roger and Nate look at me differently after finding out about my criminal past. They had a perception of me of being someone who is nice. The idea of me being some kind of criminal was a joke to them. I never told them about the history of my parents or the crappy apartment or any of the other parts of my past. I liked them not knowing about it and only thinking about how I am in the present. They thought I was a good kid, and I didn't want to do anything to change their perception of me. Shortly after the incident with the police, Roger lets me know they found someone who is a good guitar player to take my place in the band. I smile and tell him I understand. My short-lived musical career then came to an abrupt end. I keep telling myself I didn't actually lie to them, I just kept things from them. It's not the same thing.

I now understand how the truth is a formidable weapon. It can harm you when people refuse to accept it. The truth can also harm you when it's told to those who know nothing about it.

CHAPTER 18

Music and laughter and Judaism

During the school year, my mother's oldest son comes to visit. He's 16 years older than me and has been an adult since I was young. My mother's oldest son is a free spirit and Vietnam veteran. He drinks a lot, smokes a lot of weed, and is generally out of it most of the time. We both admit we are half-brothers but do not know one another. I can only remember seeing him a few times in my life. I don't think we've ever had a conversation until this visit. When I was growing up, he was busy fighting in a war and raising a family. There are no real feelings between us.

We're very different people. We are polite to one another and spend time together. He does something that does have a profoundly positive effect on my life. My half-brother gives me some popular music albums. Led Zeppelin, Pink Floyd, Deep Purple, The Who, Emerson Lake and Palmer are all artists whose albums he leaves when he returns to his home. I get back from school the day he leaves and see a note from him on top of the stack of albums. He says they're mine and to enjoy them.

I listen to the albums daily. I come home from school and do homework while listening to Pink Floyd. If I want to forget something that upset me during the day, I play Led Zeppelin. I have determined which music meets my every mood. In school, these are the bands all the kids talk about and listen to on the radio. I've finally found a way to connect to other students. They feel the same way I do about this music. It's the topic of many conversations.

My half-sister comes to visit. Her husband is a nice guy. We don't have too much of a connection, but I respect him. I get to meet my half-sister's daughter. They spend a lot of time doing things with my mother. It doesn't bother me. I enjoy having my mother's time occupied.

The day before my half-sister and her family are to return to their home, she gives me a comedy album by George Carlin from her and her husband as a belated birthday present. I thank her, but I've never heard of him before. The day my half-sister and her family leave, my mother is depressed. She tells me how she constantly misses being with her children. I just smile at her and walk away.

The first time I play the album by George Carlin, I laugh. I'm overwhelmed by the wit and logic in his humor. I feel an instant connection. I get other comedy albums by him as well as comedy albums by Cheech and Chong, Steve Martin, and others. My favorite comedy television shows are *Monty Python's Flying Circus*, *The Benny Hill Show*, *Sanford and Son*, and *All in the Family*. I read books by writers who are the masters of writing humor columns such as Erma Bombeck, Art Buchwald, and others. Comedy begins to be a strong influence in my life.

I soon learn that I have a habit of saying things before thinking exactly what I'm actually saying. It often makes teachers angry. Most kids just accept what they're told to do and accept what is asked of them without questioning it. My comedy influence helps me to see the absurdity in what is often accepted. I have no fear. My grades have never been that good and there is so much stuff on my permanent record, I believe I'm not going to college or anything like it. I have nothing to lose by cracking jokes and being funny in school.

A teacher asks me, "Are you sure you did your homework?"

I say, "It came to me in a dream that I did my homework. I sure hope it wasn't a dream. If it was, I'm in trouble. Those silly dreams can mess up a guy. Look, here it is, I wasn't dreaming. I did my homework. Boy, am I lucky."

I pull out my homework and give it to the teacher. She groans and grabs it out of my hand.

There are other times when teachers enjoy my humor.

A teacher in science class is talking about an article that describes how they tell lions from one another by counting their whiskers. She asks how we would count the whiskers on a lion. I raise my hand.

When the teacher calls on me, I say, "Very carefully."

Some kids in the class laugh and the teacher smiles. I begin to realize comedic timing is everything.

A perky girl comes into class. She's always happy and dresses nicely. She does great in the class and is just the picture of an all-around successful student. I'm in class early, and she turns around and wants to talk for some reason. She is so excited about Christmas this year. She asks me what I want. Before I realize it, I've said, "You wearing nothing but a bow under my Christmas tree. But, if you have nothing but a bow, I don't think Santa would let me have you."

The girl's face turns red. She slowly turns around and stops talking to me. I've struck a nerve. I feel bad for what I've just said. I realize I've embarrassed her. She didn't deserve it. After class, I see her at her locker and walk up to her.

I say, "I'm sorry if what I said to you before class embarrassed you. I like to tell jokes and sometimes I get carried away. I didn't mean to upset you."

She doesn't look at me and says, "It's okay."

"Hey, a pretty girl like you probably hears quite a few guys say stupid stuff like that to her."

"No, actually, you're the first."

"Oh, so you'll remember me as your first. I guess we have a special connection."

She smiles, "Okay, now how about we both get to class? All is forgiven and don't worry about it."

She closes her locker and starts to walk away.

I yell, "I hope Santa doesn't get too embarrassed when I tell him what I want for Christmas."

I realize that sometimes I can't help myself.

She turns back, laughs, and says, "Oh, stop it, will you?"

I have no idea why I said what I did to her. Before my interaction with this girl, I found her annoying. Now, as I watch her walk down the hall, I realize she is kind of pretty and is a nice girl from a good family. She was just trying to be nice to me. I hope she never learns about my past.

I soon develop a reputation with teachers and other kids for my sarcasm and humor. At times, I struggle to take things seriously. A new kid arrives at school. His name is Robbie. He used to live on Long Island, New York. I thought *I* was sarcastic and challenged teachers. I soon learned Robbie has the ability to take it to a whole new level. I admire him and we become friends.

At the end of class, our health class teacher says, "It's important to get a good grade in this class because what you do here will impact the rest of your life."

Robbie raises his hand and when called on, he says, "So, let's say I'm a brilliant mathematician who can solve problems most other people can't. Are you saying I'll be told I may be a brilliant mathematician, but because I didn't get a good grade in health class, they won't give me a job? Is this what you're telling me?"

This is a bit of a setup because Robbie excels at the most advanced math classes the school offers. When the teacher asks Robbie if he's a brilliant mathematician, he says he's probably the best in the school. He just struggles with health class. The teacher and Robbie go back and forth debating this subject until the bell rings. My admiration for Robbie only increases.

The next time we're in class, I ask Robbie if he has ever heard of George Carlin. He tells me George Carlin is one of his favorites as well as Cheech and Chong. He asks me if I like watching *Monty*

Python and *Benny Hill*. I enthusiastically say yes and describe what happened during the latest episodes of the shows. Robbie has watched them as well. We have a connection. Before and after class we talk about comedy and comedians. It's something the other kids don't seem to think about in the same way as Robbie and me.

I'm doing better in school than usual. I'm still not doing work too far above average. I don't struggle to understand things, I struggle to not be bored. This is when my mind wanders and I begin to think of funny things going on around me. I write in a notebook about how one teacher who looks like a shaven Rasputin and probably downs one too many vodkas in his free time. A member of the school administration looks to me like he has been cloned with a bulldog during a failed scientific experiment. I escape into my written world and it makes being in school more tolerable for me.

Robbie is about my height with blue eyes and fine black hair. He speaks with a thick New York accent. The girls adore him. They giggle when he's around them. They leave him mysterious notes. Some girls even walk past his house in case there is a chance they could see him. I learn that he is dating a girl who is in a higher grade. He tells me about her and says that she's a Mormon. I have no idea what that means, so I'm quiet.

I get invited to Robbie's house. He tells me to not be put off by his mother because she is a very typical New York Jewish mother. I have no idea what he's talking about, so I tell him it won't bother me.

It's a Sunday morning. Robbie and I are going bike riding on some trails I know in a wooded area at the edge of town. Robbie opens the door and tells me he has to finish cleaning up in the kitchen, and then we can go.

A short, stout woman wearing a plain dress and dark hair in a bun on the back of her head walks over to me and Robbie.

She says, "So Robbie, are you going to introduce your mother to your new friend or what? I'm not a wall decoration, you know."

Robbie introduces me to his mother. She speaks with an accent I have never heard before. Robbie then points to a man sitting on a chair in the living room reading a newspaper. He says this is his father. The newspaper slowly comes down to reveal a man smoking a pipe. He waves at me and the newspaper goes back up.

Robbie turns to his mother and says, "Ma, I'm gonna finish the dishes like you asked. Now, don't be too crazy with my friend."

"Crazy, he calls his only mother crazy. This is how he treats me. I do so much for my son, and he introduces me to his friends as crazy. God will get you for this Robbie, mark my words."

I go over and sit down on the couch.

Robbie's mother sits down in a chair across from me and says, "So, tell me, are you Jewish?"

The newspaper comes down and Robbie's father says, "Leyona, just leave the boy alone, he has only known you for a few minutes."

"Do not pay attention to that newspaper-reading man who lets his son run wild with women."

I say, "No, I don't think I'm Jewish. I've only been to church once in my life, and I got beat up when I went there."

"Would you like to be Jewish?"

This time the newspaper comes down quickly and Robbie's father says loudly, "Now stop it, Leyona. The boy didn't come over here so you could convert him to Judaism."

Leyona says, "What? He could become a Jew if he wants. Anybody can become a Jew if they want. That's how it works. It's a fair question."

Leaning his head in from the kitchen, holding a cloth as he wipes off a dish, Robbie says, "Leave it alone Ma, we're going to go bike riding, so talk about that for a while."

Leyona sighs and says to me, "Bike riding I understand, breaking a mother's heart I don't understand. Let me tell you something."

Leyona points her head toward the kitchen and yells, "You should marry a nice Jewish girl when you get older. She will make something of you. Take my husband Stanley, a garbage man at best without me."

The newspaper comes down again and Stanley says, "Leyona, leave the boy alone."

"It's true, the man lived in a place with cockroaches when I met him. Now, he lives in a nice clean home. No thanks to him."

"Leyona, I lived in New York City, lots of apartment buildings had infestation problems. They were old buildings. It takes time to get rid of those things. The building owners were trying to fix the problem. Let it go."

"All the work I do around here for my family and what happens? My husband constantly ignores me and my only son has a goy for a girlfriend. I tell you, it's not fair."

Robbie comes out of the kitchen and says to me, "Let's get out of here before my mother has arranged for your bat mitzvah."

Leyona turns to me, points to Robbie, and says, "He acts like it was such a bad thing. The boy got enough money at his bat mitzvah to buy a house—a small house, but a house. Let me ask you one more thing before you and Robbie go."

Before she can ask, Robbie and his father say in unison, "No."

Leyona acts surprised and says, "What? What was I going to say? My family, who thinks they know me so well?"

I quickly realize Robbie is by the door with it open. When I step out, he turns back to his mother and says something about her agreeing to not ask his male friends questions about their circumcisions.

Robbie and I become friends. I introduce him to my parents and my mother is nice and my dad acts friendly. My parents have changed a lot over the years. I constantly talk about humor and comedy with Robbie. I soon discover he also likes to write stories. He explains it's a struggle because his father is an engineer and his sister is away at college studying to be a physicist. Math is considered something almost sacred in his home. He must do his math homework every night and his father always checks it. Writing is something he can only do when he gets some free time, and he doesn't often have much of it.

I offer him some of my stories to read. When Robbie eventually reads them, I'm surprised he likes them. I then read some of his stories and realize he's got a gift for writing science fiction. His stories always have a bit of humor in them and I think they're good.

I believe he is a better writer than I am, but I don't care. Robbie is such a great friend.

I think Robbie's mother is one of the funniest people I've ever met in my life. I often do imitations of her for Robbie. He can't control himself laughing. One time, I'm over at Robbie's house. I'm behind his mother imitating her walk. Robbie and his father are trying not to laugh.

When she turns around and sees me, Leyona says, "I like you, but sometimes, you can be such a yutz."

I learn about Jewish traditions and things Robbie has to do because he's Jewish. One day, Leyona asks me if I'd like to go to a bris with their family. When I look past Leyona, Robbie and his father are behind moving their arms to stop me. I tell Leyona I can't go. She says it is a shame because it would have been a good opportunity for me to meet some nice Jewish girls. Later, Robbie tells me all about a bris. I have to thank him for helping me avoid it.

Right before the start of the next school year, Robbie and his family move back to Long Island, New York. It is a sad day for me when they leave. Leyona hugs me and tells me I need to visit them in New York, so she can introduce me to a nice Jewish girl. Robbie and I promise to keep in touch. We write down each other's addresses, so we won't forget. He has my phone number and Robbie says he'll call when he gets his new phone number.

We keep in touch for a few months after they leave. The time between our communication starts to become longer and longer. We eventually fade out of each other's lives. I'm just relieved nobody told them about my past. If they did, Robbie never said anything to me about it. I miss my friend, but I realize I miss lots of friends. It's never easy to move on, but I'm getting better at it.

CHAPTER 19

Working Man Blues

I made enough money from my criminal activities that it lasts me for a long time. My parents pay for anything associated with being in school as well as lunch. Anything to do with spending money is up to me. I've come to realize my funds are getting low and it is probably time for me to get a job. Selling stolen items is an easy way to make a lot of money, but I don't want that to be part of my life again. I look in the newspaper and discover there is a job opening for a busboy at a restaurant. It isn't too far from where I live.

I call the number for the job and arrange to go to the restaurant that night. I ride my bike there and meet the restaurant staff and the owner. The pay is $1.50 an hour. My job is to clean off dirty tables, get things the cook needs from the back, wash dishes, and clean the kitchen before I leave at night.

After working one night, I get hired. The restaurant is so busy some days, I can barely keep up with washing all the dirty dishes. The cook is always yelling for some vegetable, bread, or meat for me to get him. When the restaurant closes at night, it seems to take a long time to finish washing all the dishes and clean the kitchen. When I walk out of the restaurant, I'm exhausted.

With working the weekends and after school, I manage to average 20 hours a week at the restaurant. My weekly take-home pay is $22.50. When I look at my first check, I remember being paid sixty dollars in Sacramento to deliver a package. I've shoplifted for less than an hour and been able to get forty dollars from someone for what I took from the store. Selling items that were stolen out of cars sometimes got me seventy-five dollars a night. I made quite a bit more money and spent a lot less time working at it. I guess crime does pay, but it also comes with some serious career hazards. I resign myself to this reality. Getting honest money eliminates the chances of facing the police. This is the main thing that motivates me to continue working at the restaurant.

One night I am getting ready to leave when the owner sees me. He tells me to stay in the dining room until he puts something in his car. On the desk at the check-out counter is a huge stack of money. It is just sitting there on the desk. Twenties, tens, fives, and one-dollar bills all in neat stacks. When I see it, I tell myself he's not going to miss a few of those bills. I then quickly shake my head and turn away. It is such a struggle. I keep telling myself I don't steal, I'm an honest person now. The owner trusts me, and I can't let him down. I keep telling myself I'm better than my past. The internal struggle is real but eventually passes.

The owner comes back inside the restaurant and smiles. He asks me to help him put the money in the night deposit bag. I keep telling myself that at least I got to touch some of that money. As we walk out, he thanks me for my hard work that day. It's dark out, and I have a light on my bike for the ride home. I then make the journey to my house through the quiet neighborhoods around the town. I avoid the main street and all the people drinking in the bars. The drunks are always doing stupid things, and I don't want to deal with them.

When the weather gets too cold, my father gets up in the middle of the night and comes to the restaurant to get me. It's the first time I can remember him being supportive of me in doing something. It feels strange, but I am thankful for his help.

I take my checks and open a bank account. The amount of money I'm making is so small, but I refuse to be discouraged. I soon learn there are a lot of larcenies committed at the restaurant by other employees.

I walk out one night to see a cook taking a box of steaks and putting them in his car. He turns around when he sees me, smiles, and puts his index finger in front of his lips signaling for me to be quiet. One waitress accuses another waitress of stealing her tips. The restaurant owner gets them calmed down. I'm told this particular waitress has a history of occasionally taking other tips that don't belong to her. The cleaning woman who opens the restaurant often puts canned goods in her car. I refuse to do anything even close to stealing. I mind my business and do my work. The other workers in the restaurant seem to think I'm quiet and shy. It's the first time in my life I've ever been considered to be this way.

Things are going well. I'm not making much money, but I am saving for an electric typewriter. I can now purchase Christmas gifts with my own money this year and that makes me happy.

Then the worst possible thing happens. They hire a new busboy. I greet him and start showing him the things to do around the restaurant. He's a nice kid, and we work together well.

One day when we're alone, he says, "Don't you remember me?"

"No, I don't remember you," I respond.

The kid laughs.

"Think juvenile hall. Does that ring a bell?"

I then recognize him and I'm too upset to move. His name is Allen, and I knew him the month I spent in juvenile hall years ago. I don't know what to say.

I plead with him, saying, "Hey, I don't want anybody here to know about that time in my life. Please don't tell anyone."

Allen laughs again.

"Oh, don't worry. Nobody will know anything. It's okay."

It appears he's been arrested again since our time in juvenile hall. I ask him not to share the details with me. He asks me if I want to go drinking when we're done working at the restaurant. I tell him maybe next time. As I ride my bike home that night, I feel sick to my stomach. I am so frustrated. All I need is a break from my history. I need people to only think of me as the person I am now. I don't want to be judged by the person I was in the past.

Things are okay with Allen for a few weeks. Then he shows up to work after drinking. He is not doing a good job. The owner asks him to go into his office to talk with him. I'm standing by the door and hear loud voices.

"What do you mean I have to go home? I ain't drunk. This is because you want to pick on a rehabilitated criminal trying to turn his life around," says Allen.

"I think it would be best if you went home. You are clearly not able to do your job tonight," says the owner.

"Hey, you treat Mark like this? He's a criminal too. He and I were best buddies in juvenile hall. You ever send him home and not pay him?"

"He's never given us a reason for it. Now please just go home."

When Allen comes out of the office, he looks at me and says, "Ain't this some shit?"

I just turn and walk away.

Things change for me at the restaurant after that day. The owner has a talk with me in his office. He is angry I didn't tell him about my time in juvenile hall. I ask if he would've hired me if I had told him. The owner says that's not the point. He tells me I can keep my job at the restaurant for now.

News like a person's criminal history travels fast among the restaurant staff. Everyone at the restaurant soon knows about my past. Some look at me differently and others treat me differently. I realize I've been found guilty of being a thief by others without anyone asking my side of things. Nobody seems to realize I've not done anything bad during my time working at the restaurant. My job eventually comes to a horrible end.

A week after the incident with Allen, I'm in the kitchen and almost finished cleaning up.

A waitress comes in and yells, "Julie had some money taken from her purse. Did you, do it?"

I yell back, "No."

"I don't believe you. I want to see what you have in your pockets."

"Go to hell."

"I'm calling the police."

I turn out my pockets and I have absolutely nothing in them.

"See, I have nothing in my pockets."

The waitress walks toward me and says, "If I find out you're lying to me. I won't bother with the police. I'll take care of you myself. I hate thieves."

"Then you must hate yourself. I've seen you take entire cheesecakes from the outside freezer and put them in your car after I closed the restaurant. Kiss my ass, you asshole bitch," I scream.

The waitress goes to grab me, and I push her back. Another waitress sticks her head in the kitchen and says she's leaving, and they have to get going now. The waitress who yelled at me says something about me watching myself. I finish cleaning the kitchen and leave.

I get a call from the restaurant owner the next day. He tells me he thinks it's best if I don't come back. I tell him I understand. My parents are disappointed with the loss of my first job. My father asks me what happened. I tell him the job was harming my school work. He says I did the right thing then. It's best to tell my parents a lie they can understand. Being honest with them would involve a price I'm not willing to pay.

My next employment experience is short-lived, but I have a great time. It appears Neil's father knows the owners of a traveling circus. They need some workers when they come to town. I'm asked if I would like to work with the circus for the time, they're in town. It seems like a fun experience and I agree.

The circus arrives, and Neil and I show up ready to do whatever is asked of us. He is going to be selling popcorn, and I am going to be selling cotton candy. I spend hours every night traipsing up and down wooden bleachers yelling about cotton candy. Neil and I get there early the next day and the owners of the circus introduce us to the performers and let us see the animals. I'm fascinated.

After a week, the circus leaves. During the time I worked for the circus, I sold popcorn, cotton candy, soda drinks, and hot dogs. I make much more money than at the restaurant. I know it is only temporary, but I'm told if I'm available next year when they come around, they'd like me to work with them. I tell them I'd love it. I had a great time.

During my time with the circus, I develop a crush on a girl who is my age and a trapeze performer. One day a tent flap is open and

I see the girl practicing her trapeze routine. I enjoy watching her practice. I work up the nerve to say hello to her one day after this. She comes over and asks if I'd like to be a trapeze artist. I'm invited to come one day when she is practicing and I can try it. My fear of doing the trapeze is greater than my crush. The circus leaves before I go back to try to see her again.

After the circus, I get a job selling programs at local college basketball games. It's an easy job. I never have any problems. People come up, pay the money, and I give them a program. It's so simple but things get tense for me one day.

I'm standing at the entrance selling programs. A man takes a program from me and doesn't pay. I keep telling him the program is seventy-five cents. The man just looks at me, smiles, and keeps walking.

I walk after him and say, "Are you going to pay the seventy-five cents for the program or not? If not, I want the program back."

Again, the man just smiles at me and says nothing. I take the program from his hand and walk back to my spot at the entrance. Before I get there, another man grabs the program from me and then grabs the front of my shirt.

He says, "Do you know who that is who you just disrespected over a stupid basketball program?"

I make the guy let me go and say, "Yeah, some guy who tried to steal a program from me. That's who he is to me."

The man leans in closer and tells me the guy's son is a professional football player. He is one of the top players in the NFL. I tell him I don't care. The programs are seventy-five cents, and I wasn't told of any discounts for people with offspring who play in the NFL.

He grabs me again and I then grab him. The next thing I know, my boss is between us. After he hears what I have to say and what the guy has to say, he simply hands the man a program and apologizes. I'm stunned.

"What was all that about? You made me look like an idiot," I say.

My boss responds, "Hey, you have to understand that man has a lot of pull in our community. We don't need him to be angry at us."

"What is he going to do? Have his NFL son come and tell everyone not to buy our programs at the basketball game? Hey, if his son is an NFL player, seventy-five cents should be something easy for him to pay."

"I hope you realize we need people to advertise in our programs. If word gets out that we upset him, it could discourage potential advertisers from using us."

"That's ridiculous."

"No, that's reality."

I sell programs until the last basketball game of the season. I don't know if I'll be back to do it next year. When I am finished with my jobs, I have enough money to last me for a while. The experience makes me realize there is a fine line between right and wrong. It's a line that always becomes blurred based on what a person needs to be true. Reality is often not all that important.

C H A P T E R   2 0

Seeing Stars

I am a young child playing Little League and baseball is my world. I play baseball during my games, during practice, and every time I see a pick-up baseball game being played in the neighborhood. My room is filled with baseball cards, posters of baseball players, baseball magazines, as well as baseball equipment.

I'm not alone. Other kids my age love the game of baseball in the same way. We watch the games on television, listen to them on the radio, and read about them in the daily newspapers. It is something we talk about often. One of the kids from my Little League team enjoys going to see the professionals play. There is a city not too far from where we live, and it has a Major League Baseball team. When I do get the opportunity to go and see the professional team play, I go with his family.

My friends and I spend our time at these baseball games sitting in the stands with our baseball gloves on our hands, wearing our baseball hats as we cheer for the home team. When the night is over, our stomachs are filled with hot dogs, popcorn, and soda. The experience provides each of us with a special sense of exhilaration. We often walk back to the family's car talking about our future baseball careers. My friend and I believe our future as professional baseball players will be filled with legendary accomplishments. In our minds, it is just a matter of time.

I go with my friend's family to a game where some players will be available to sign autographs when it is over. As we read about it in the program, we realize one of our favorite players will be signing autographs, his name is Roberto Clemente. My friend and I are about as excited as any young boys would be who have a chance to meet their sports idol.

It's a good game. Going into the bottom of the ninth, the game is tied three to three. A player from our team hits a home run with two men on base. They win the game six to three. It is very exciting to watch.

After the game, we go to the area outside the baseball stadium where the players are signing autographs. Many people are offering their programs for the players to sign, others have autograph books, and some just have scraps of paper. My friend and I wait patiently in line. I see Roberto Clemente, and I am so excited to be so close to him I can't speak. It seems like forever, but eventually, only a few people are in front of us. The line to see Roberto Clemente is moving slowly. He is taking his time and speaking with people.

Suddenly a security guard comes out, gets in front of Roberto Clemente, and faces the crowd.

"I'm sorry folks, the time for signing autographs is over. These guys have played an entire game and are pretty tired. There will be some other players here for tomorrow's game, he says.

There is a collective groan from the crowd. My friend and I are dumbfounded and don't know what to do. We were so close. I then hear Roberto Clemente speak to the security guard.

He talks in his thick Puerto Rican accent and says, "Das okay man, I sign, I still sign, it's okay. Day here waiting for us an is okay."

The security guard says, "Okay Mr. Clemente, but we have to get things going here real soon."

Roberto Clemente then continues to sign baseball programs as well as other things and talk to people. When it is our turn, my friend goes first. Roberto Clemente asks my friend if he likes baseball, and my friend says he loves baseball. Roberto Clemente tells him he is glad to hear it and hopes he always likes baseball. When it is my turn, I am in awe of being next to Roberto Clemente. I've watched him play baseball on television. I've listened to him play on the radio. I have read about him in baseball magazines. I even have his baseball card. I can't speak and simply hand him my baseball program. Roberto Clemente takes the baseball program and smiles at me.

As he's signing it, he says, "You like to play baseball?"

I nod my head up and down as the ability to engage in verbal speech has momentarily left me.

He then says, "Das good, maybe someday you come here and play on my team with me."

I nod my head up and down and smile. Roberto Clemente then smiles and pats my shoulder. The people behind us are anxious to see him, and I'm quickly pushed out of the way.

On the drive home, I don't talk too much. I keep replaying in my mind what Roberto Clemente had said to me and that he had touched my shoulder. I can't stop staring at his signature on my baseball program. My friend can't wait to tell the other kids on our Little League team about seeing Roberto Clemente. I can't stop reliving the moment in my mind.

When I get home, I get my Roberto Clemente baseball cards, I get baseball magazines that have articles about him. I place them with the baseball program that was signed by Roberto Clemente in a special place in my bedroom. I have created my own little display of Roberto Clemente memorabilia.

It was 1972 when Roberto Clemente died in a plane crash. He was delivering supplies to people who were victims of an earthquake. When I learned of his death, I cried like someone who had lost a loved one. I never knew Roberto Clemente beyond a few seconds spent getting his autograph. I'll always remember him as a well-known professional athlete who gave a young boy struggling with a terrible home life a few seconds of feeling special. He provided a cherished memory consisting of kind words that would be held onto and thought about in happy as well as upsetting times. He may not have known me, but I know I will never be able to forget him.

School is over for the year. Different people in my grade have gotten their driving permits and some have gotten their driver's licenses. I don't turn 16 until the end of the summer, so I have to wait. My friends and I have moved beyond bicycles and now have incorporated the use of the public bus system in our travel agendas. It's a time of struggle for all my friends as they want more independence from their parents. Our battles with parents are often the topic of many conversations among us.

One of the things that is often talked about is going to concerts. I have been to some small ones with my friends and their families. I have a friend named Fred who will have a birthday in a week. His mother is going to purchase tickets for him and two of his friends to go and see a concert. When Fred asks if I'd like to go, I am excited. It will be my first time going to a huge concert at a stadium in the city. The excitement is only increased as his mother says if it is okay with our parents, we can go to the concert by ourselves using the public bus. My parents don't care, and Sam's parents are okay with it as long as there are three of us going together.

On the day of the concert, I show up at Fred's house. His mother has a cooler of drinks and sandwiches prepared for us to take. It's Styrofoam and a little heavy. We don't care; it is filled with great stuff to drink and eat.

We get on a bus heading toward the city. It is filled with kids our age and older going to the concert. This is the biggest concert any of us have been to before. Our only other concert experiences involved hearing local bands in school gymnasiums or at high school sports fields. This one will take place where the professional athletes play. It can hold tens of thousands of people.

When the three of us get to the stadium, there is the smell of marijuana everywhere. People are selling pills and others are drinking all types of alcohol. Fred says we probably look like little kids going to a concert. Here we are in a big city with a Styrofoam cooler filled with sandwiches, fried chicken, and sodas. I tell him I don't care; I like not needing to pay for food. Sam agrees and as we walk with the Styrofoam cooler. All of us are as protective of it as if we are transporting the holy grail.

Sam doesn't want any of us to eat anything from the cooler until we get inside the stadium. It takes some serious negotiations from me and Sam to get a soda and a sandwich as we wait for the concert to start.

We hear some noise that sounds like a gate opening. We get to the front of the line. We don't realize it at the moment, but this turns out to be a huge mistake. At large concerts with tens of thousands of people waiting to get inside, there is quite a bit of pushing by people from behind. It is a powerful force and not easy to handle. When the gates are completely open, we can feel the tremendous pressure from the surge of people behind us. Sam screams that if we don't lift the cooler over our heads, it will break. We struggle to get the cooler up, but the pressure from the crowd is just too strong. At this time, I start swearing, Sam starts swearing, Fred starts swearing, and the people around us start swearing. We're being moved from side to side and the pressure from the back only increases. We can only take little steps toward the gate. Once we're about to get through the gate, we hear a crack. Sam, Fred, and I are screaming at one another. When we're about to get in the stadium, the Styrofoam cooler breaks and the food and drinks go everywhere. Sam and I keep Fred from leaning down to try to pick up anything, we're afraid he could get run over.

We get inside and look back to see people kicking the cans of soda and stepping on the food. None of us know what to do now. We are all heartbroken and angry at the loss of the cooler. Sam says his mother will kill him—she got that cooler special just for today. She was so excited to get it ready for the concert. We agree not to tell her, but say the cooler got broken in an accident once we got inside the stadium. We plan to say all the food and drinks she provided were great. Sam agrees that is the only thing we can do about it. This will make her happy. I guess sometimes telling lies can help protect people's feelings. I figure I'm not going to tell Sam's mother anything.

We make our way to our seats. As we sit there, clouds of marijuana smoke come our way from many directions. We try to brush it away, but we begin to feel the effects. Fred and I tell Sam we're going to get some food for all of us. He doesn't have to pay since he tried to bring the cooler.

It is a special time sitting in a huge stadium, packed with people listening to Aerosmith, Foghat, and others. We can't stop laughing when we realize our eyes are now pink. A fight breaks out behind me and when I look back a guy comes tumbling down beside me. Another guy comes down in hot pursuit. People come from all sides go to the fight and try to break it up. This lasts for about twenty minutes. The entire time, Sam, Fred, and I just sit there calmly watching people right next to us brawling. It seems as if the concert music is background music for the fight. When it's all over, Sam, Fred, and I look at each other and can't stop laughing.

All three of us soon learn that after a huge concert like the one we attended; public buses are often full. We keep waiting and waiting, but the buses that come past are too filled to hold any more people in them. We don't know what time we will get home or even if we will get home.

One of the public buses stops at a red light. A back window opens and it's Roger.

He waves to us and says, "Hey, come on, get in, it's crazy out there."

We all look at one another and then run to the bus. Sam is the first one pulled through the window, and I'm next. The bus starts to move when it's Fred's turn. We are pulling Fred into the bus as it is making a turn. He is hanging on as the bus turns, and he makes it. Once inside, nobody can figure out how to close the window of the bus. It moves in and out the entire time we are on our way home.

Once we get back to the town, Roger asks if we all want to go to his place. When we are there, Sam calls his mother. She told him to call her no matter what the time. She is on her way to pick us up and take us home. I admire Sam's relationship with his mother. He is so special to her.

Before Sam's mother arrives, Roger sits down next to me.

He says, "Hey, why haven't you been coming around for such a long time? We miss you, man."

"Well, you guys seemed pretty upset when you learned about all the stuff I've done. I figured I made you guys uncomfortable, so I just stayed away," I responded.

"Aw, man, sorry about the miscommunication. It just surprised us is all. We just never knew anybody who is so well-known by the police. Hey, how about you start coming around again? We always have plenty of beers somewhere."

"Okay, I hope you don't need a guitar player for your band. I may not be the best choice."

"Don't worry, we got it covered. Your musical talents are not required by us at the moment. We may need you to keep Nate from getting arrested."

We share a laugh, and I hear Sam say his mother has arrived. I feel good about having this talk with Roger.

When I arrive home, I quietly go upstairs and to my bedroom. I lay awake and realize nothing is how you think it would be. I thought this concert would be calm and reserved like the ones I had been to around town. It was a completely different experience. I thought Roger didn't want me around because of my past. I was wrong. I had planned in my mind a million things I was going to say to Roberto Clemente before I met him. I never thought I'd be too excited to speak. I tell myself no matter how much I think I know; I still have a lot to learn.

CHAPTER 21

A Rite of Passage and Dodgeball

I know there are many things' parents don't look forward to as their child gets older. Some worry about their child's body developing properly. Others fear their child learning how to socialize with the opposite sex. It seems one of the greatest fears all parents have is the anxiety associated with their child becoming old enough to drive. This driving experience begins with getting a learner's permit.

I get my learner's permit for driving shortly after my sixteenth birthday. It has been years since I saw my father so stressed. I'm not sure if the thought of teaching me to drive is causing him any more anxiety than being a soldier in World War II. After seeing the look on his face, I bet it's close.

My parents aren't certain I need a driver's license. I provide them with a spirited argument in favor of me driving. I tell them it's simple. My father can have time off from taking my mother to the store and other places. If I have a driver's license, I can take her where she wants to go. I know it is a solid argument. I'm actually motivated to drive because I want to be able to pick up my friends and go to the mall or to see drive-in movies with certain girls. Being alone with girls in a car is a major motivation of mine. After a few days, they agree I should have a driver's license.

I then go to the DMV with my father, take my eye exam, get a booklet about driving laws and regulations, then submit my application for a driving permit. It is after this happens that I start to check the mail daily. I even wait for the postman to deliver our mail on some days. When school starts, this is no longer possible.

The day arrives when I get my driver's permit. I can't wait to begin driving. My father agrees to take me out. I feel so different sitting in the driver's seat of my dad's car with the steering wheel in front of me. My father starts telling me things about driving and all I can think about is what girls I want to take to see a drive-in movie.

I think I should have listened more to what my father had been trying to tell me. Things don't go well my first time behind the wheel of a car. Starting the car is fine, then I pull out onto the road. My father tells me I almost hit the car on the right, I almost hit the car coming at us, I'm taking a turn too wide, I'm not far enough from the centerline. So, after two blocks, I give up and my father takes over driving for the day. He says maybe we can continue after I have some driving classes at school.

The driving class in school is done by a man who calmly repeats himself. He does this when teaching how to drive, in the classroom, and even in general conversation if you interrupt him. The classroom portion of the driving class is not complicated, and it covers what we need to know to take the driving test. Going out to learn to drive with this teacher proves to be quite interesting.

Because of his habit of repeating himself, we give the teacher the nickname of Mr. Mr. Slowdown Slowdown. It seems you are often told to slow down by him when driving the school's car even if it seems you're not going too fast. During some classes, we meet Mr. Mr. Slowdown Slowdown at a school car in the parking lot for our driving class.

The first day this happens, a kid named Doug is chosen to drive. Mr. Mr. Slowdown Slowdown is sitting in the front passenger seat. He has a brake pedal on this side to stop the car if necessary. Doug enjoys driving, but he enjoys talking even more. He almost goes through a stop sign, but Mr. Mr. Slowdown Slowdown stops the car before this happens. Doug starts to get a lecture and keeps talking and driving. Mr. Mr. Slowdown Slowdown begins to repeat what he has said from the beginning because Doug interrupts him. It is a bit annoying as we drive along and Doug keeps talking about anything and everything, Mr. Mr. Slowdown Slowdown keeps repeating what he said at the beginning of the driving class. We are occasionally jolted forward because Doug seems to have no idea you have to stop at stop signs and Mr. Mr. Slowdown Slowdown has to make a hard stop from the passenger side.

Eventually, it's my turn to drive. I don't talk and just drive. I let Mr. Mr. Slowdown Slowdown talk and I do okay. He says some things I didn't realize and because I don't interrupt him, I only hear them once when I drive. The last person to drive is a girl who is almost brought to tears when Mr. Mr. Slowdown Slowdown has to use the brake because she doesn't judge a red light properly. Driving class is a rather unique experience.

I am slowly getting better at driving. I know I'm improving when my father seems to breathe normally when we're out together practicing my driving. Every day after school, we drive around town and on open highways. He tells me to take on various driving challenges. I get better and my confidence is high. I tell myself I'm ready to take the driving test.

There is one thing that is not in my favor with taking the driving test. My father's car is not in the best shape. It will stall in certain situations, doesn't have power steering or power brakes, and is old. My father is saving money for a new car and won't have one for a few more months. I still decide to take the driver's test.

On my first attempt at the driving test, I fail. The written part is easy for me. I'm quite nervous and when my father's car stalls during the test, I just can't think. I wait a while and take the test again. I fail again. This time my father's car stalls twice; the second time my father has to come out and fix it during my test. I'm frustrated, embarrassed, and I don't know what I can do to change things. My father says maybe I shouldn't drive. I walk away before I say something about not being required to drive his beat-up old car for my driving test.

My half-sister arrives for a visit. They have a car that is only a few years old. It is a beautiful car. I ask my half-sister's husband if I could take my driving exam in his car. I'm surprised when he agrees. He is a soft-spoken man who is always calm. On my way to take the driving test, his demeanor makes me calm. His car has power brakes, power steering, and is very comfortable. I feel I could drive it forever.

Since his car is from out of state, there are questions from those administering the test. My half-sister's husband smiles as he answers all of their questions and provides them with all the required paperwork. I can take my driving test using his car.

Before I go out for my driving test, my half-sister's husband says, "I think you'll do fine."

I've never had anybody give me reassurance like this before, and it feels great. I take the driving test and get the highest marks. I can't believe it. I'm finally a licensed driver. I drive home and can't thank my half-sister's husband enough. He is very polite and tells me he is glad to have been able to help me. I've never experienced anyone like him before in a family setting. I'm overwhelmed with emotion.

My father comes home from the bar. He played golf during the day and was at a local bar with his friends. When he hears I have my driver's license, he tells me he didn't know if I had what it took to be a driver, but he's glad I have my license. His comments make me angry, but I ask for the keys to his car and my father gives them to me. I just drive around town and go to a store. I see some people I know and tell them about getting my driver's license, and they're excited for me. It takes me a few days to get over the excitement.

The next time I'm driving the school's car for class, Mr. Mr. Slowdown Slowdown tells me I should consider taking my driver's test. I tell him I have my license. He then begins to tell me about things I should know since I got my license. I don't interrupt him; I don't want him to start from the beginning of his talk as I know he will.

My daily routine now includes going to school and writing my stories at home. Sometimes I will see a friend. My life doesn't have much excitement. I'm trying to stay out of trouble. The occasional nudge by a jock after gym class is ignored by me. Comments made behind my back about my mother are something I've learned to also ignore. I'm getting better at controlling my temper. My grades are still not too far above average. I wish someone in the school could understand how boring I find everything. Something tells me I'm not the only one who has this feeling.

Now that I'm in the upper grades, we can play dodgeball in gym class. The nerds and the greasers are usually wiped out at the beginning of the game. This will then leave the jocks to battle it out to win a game. I am the exception—an unclassified student who is not good at school, doesn't play sports, and has no mechanical ability. I am the outlier student of my high school. I'm also good at dodgeball.

Our gym teacher believes having a dodgeball tournament between the different classes is a good thing. It goes as predicted. Nobody but the jocks seem to enjoy playing the game. They are the ones who tend to dominate every aspect of the tournament. I am on a team that advances.

A kid from my old baseball team is now a top athlete in high school, and before we start a game, he whispers something about my mother as we're standing in line. When I look at him, he laughs. I'm motivated to do whatever it takes to win.

This game determines what team goes to the championship. It is a tough game that is close. Many people are trying to hit me in the head, but I avoid it. This is something that shouldn't be done, but those responsible usually claim they didn't mean for it to happen. They're warned not to do it again, but they do the same thing.

The game now comes down to me and the kid from my old baseball team. He is smiling and telling his teammate on the side that this will be an easy win. I don't have the arm strength he does, so I try to spin the ball as I throw it, hoping it will pop out of his hands. He easily avoids the ball.

Then it's his turn to throw the dodgeball at me. He runs up to the line, jumps up, and when he releases the ball, it comes sailing at a high velocity through the air toward my head. I dive, hit the floor, and barely escape being hit. His teammates think this is quite funny. He doesn't realize I've figured him out. I know when he'll release the ball and where he'll throw it. I just need him to throw it at my head one more time.

I go up to the line and intentionally give a lousy throw that misses him. His teammates again laugh and urge me to just give up. My teammates are trying to encourage me.

Just like before, he runs up to the line, jumps up and when he lands, he throws the dodgeball with tremendous speed right at my head. This time I jump up and catch the ball as it hits my stomach. I stagger a little when I land. I've just had the wind knocked out of me. I still hold onto the ball and my team wins the game. We're going to be in the championship.

I hear his teammate asking him how he could let a freak like me win. I go to the centerline and carefully place the ball down.

I look at him and say, "Nice game."

He's angry and gives me the middle finger and says, "Yeah asshole, sit and spin."

Nothing is worse for a jock than losing any type of game. It can be made worse if you lose a game to a kid, you consider insignificant and beneath you. Being taunted by his teammates only makes things worse for him.

When we get out of the locker room, I'm heading to class. Other kids are coming into the gym for their class. The guy from my old baseball team grabs my shoulder and turns me around to face him.

He points his finger at me and says, "What you did today was some bullshit. Don't you know your place in this world?"

I yell, "What are you talking about? So, you lost and it's time to get over it."

I try to leave and he grabs me again.

"Listen, you little pimple on my ass, I think you owe me an apology."

"For what? Being able to handle a dodgeball you threw at my head?"

"Look, if you don't apologize right now, you know what I'm going to do to you?"

I don't want to fight. I don't want to get into trouble. It is a tremendous struggle to keep my temper under control. The next thing I know a senior from the football team comes up and puts his arm around the shoulders of my adversary.

He says, "You're going to plead for him to have sex with your mother because your father is tired of it."

There is laughter from the guys who are standing around us.

"Hey, Bart, you know we can't let lowlifes like this disrespect us in front of people. He's got to be taught a lesson."

"The only lesson you're teaching him is how to deal with your bad breath. Now, get out of here and forget about it. You got more important stuff with the football team to worry about than this. So, get out of here and stay out of trouble. We need you on the team."

Bart is a tall, strong, and large kid. I don't know what to say. After the guys leave, he comes up and introduces himself. I notice his last name is familiar.

"Do you know Victor? His dad works in the pickle factory. You both have the same last name," I say.

Bart smiles.

"Yeah, that's my little cousin. I know you because he talks about you sometimes. Just forget about this and go on to your next class. He's not a bad guy. His father just can't accept it if he loses at anything. It's a family thing."

I walk away feeling overwhelmed. The time I tried to defend Victor I thought had been a disaster. With a cousin this size, I now know why Victor didn't need my help. I think about how it's interesting the way things you put in motion by your actions impact your life. It is possible for them to come back to you in a positive way.

CHAPTER 22

Rejections and More Rejection

I walk around at school and look at all the kids who are now couples. When I see them walk down the hall hand in hand or arm in arm, I am envious. I haven't even come close to having a girlfriend since Jenny. It wasn't a good experience. A very strange experience, but not a good one.

I'm over at my friend Tim's house, and we're talking about the depression associated with not having a girlfriend. His older sister is going to college and overhears what we're saying. Her name is Betty, and she's an upbeat and energetic person. Betty tells us the girls our age are just as lonely as us. They want boyfriends just as much as we want girlfriends. We just need to learn how to approach them.

Betty looks at me and says, "So, tell me how you approach a girl you want to go out with you. What do you say?"

"Ah, well, ah, to be honest, I've never really asked a girl out on a date yet."

"So, you've never had a girlfriend?"

"Well, I guess I have."

"Well, how did you ask her out on a date?"

"Ah, well, a friend of mine shoved a phone at me with her on the other end. We started talking. I then hopped on a train to her house. Her father looked at me like I was strange when I jumped off and rolled in the dirt a little in front of their home. It wasn't my fault; the train was going a bit faster than I realized. That's how it happened. I didn't actually ask her out on a date or anything."

I know hearing honesty is never easy, but Betty is making it difficult by looking at me as if I am strange. She is doing this more than Jenny's father did. I feel uncomfortable.

"Okay, we'll come back to you," she says.

Tim then talks about his old girlfriend named Margaret. He tells Betty about how he and Margaret used to like reading comic books together. They met each other while standing at a store reading comics. Margaret liked comics such as *Richie Rich, Wendy the Witch, Mighty Mouse,* and others like them. Tim said he likes comics like *Spiderman, Superman, The Avengers,* and other similar types of comics. They discussed who is the best comic book character and that's how they met. Tim explains how they both liked drinking root beer, eating hamburgers, and watching cartoons on television.

Betty says, "Okay, we see you know how to spend time with girls. So, tell me, why did you guys break up with your girlfriends?"

I went first and said, "Well, my girlfriend wanted me to steal her grandmother's bracelet from her old boyfriend. I didn't want to do it. because I didn't want to go to juvenile hall for breaking into someone's house. She got really angry at me when I refused to steal her grandmother's bracelet from her old boyfriend's house. That's when she broke up with me."

"What was her grandmother's bracelet doing in her old boyfriend's house?"

"I don't know."

"That's the only reason she broke up with you?"

"Yeah, that made her really mad."

"You're better off without her."

I think to myself that Betty is right, but I'm also really lonely without Jenny.

Tim says he got into an argument with his girlfriend because she liked watching cartoons, he told her are made for babies. She got angry at him. He said the comics she liked to read are also for babies. She told him to take it back, and when he refused, she told him to get out of her house and never come back. He says he doesn't miss her and her inability to appreciate the seriousness of comics. He doesn't understand how anyone would want to be with her once they find out about the comics she likes to read.

Betty looks at both of us and seems stunned.

"I see I have much work to do here," she says.

Tim and I get encouragement from Betty for what seems to be a very long time. She tells us we should show some confidence and ask out a girl. Betty says if we are confident and nice, a girl will go on a date with us. I soon leave and my friend is envious of me. He has to stay with his sister because his family is about to have dinner. As I drive back to my house, I bet Tim is getting more girlfriend lectures from his sister.

I think about what Betty said. I have a girl in mind. She is a rather attractive blonde with the name of Terri. This girl is shy and hates going to school as much as I do. I figure we have plenty to talk about.

After lunch, I see her walking down the hall. I walk quickly and get beside her. My throat is dry, and I'm nervous. Terri just keeps walking and I keep walking beside her trying to work up the nerve to ask her to the movies. Suddenly, she stops and looks at me.

"Do you want something? Why are you walking next to me?" says Terri.

I clear my throat and try to remain calm. My heart is about to beat out of my chest.

"I'd like to know if you, ah, you know, ah, would, kinda, you know, like to, ah go to the movies, ah this Saturday. I mean I'll pay and all. So, ah, Saturday is good for you? Is that okay?"

Terri is a pretty girl whose face shows sheer utter disgust.

"No, no way in hell I'd go on a date with you. I have no idea who would want to go on a date with you. Now, go away and leave me alone," says Terri.

She then walks very fast toward her next class.

I feel so embarrassed and hurt. I try to act like it's nothing by calmly walking to my next class. I go from being sad to being angry, and then back to serious depression. Betty told me if it doesn't work out with one girl, I should try another.

I decide not to give up. I then figure I'll ask a girl named Sonya to the movies. After class is over, every person is gone from the classroom except for me and her. I look at Sonya and say, "Hey, ah, would you, kinda, sorta, maybe, like to go with me to, ah, the movies this Saturday? I mean, I'll pay and everything. All you actually have to do is sit there and watch the movie. It's no problem."

Sonya looks at me and laughs. Then she seems to think about it and then laughs even more.

Sonya says, "I don't think so."

She then walks quickly out of the classroom.

I spend the next few days wondering what is wrong with me.

Next week I'm in class with Neil. He looks around and whispers to me that Gretchen in the next row has a crush on me. I tell him not to make fun of me. I've been turned down and laughed at by girls recently, and I am in no mood to play around. He says his sister talks to her and said that Gretchen has a crush on me. I refuse to believe it. I look over at her, and she smiles at me and looks away.

Neil says, "You should ask her out."

"No, I don't believe you." I say.

"Trust me, she likes you."

"What's wrong with her?"

"Nothing, just ask her out."

Neil won't let it go, and I'm getting angry. I reach my breaking point. When class is over, I turn to Gretchen.

I say, "Hey, Gretchen, you would probably never want to go out on a date with me, right?"

Gretchen's eyes open wide. She notices all the girls and guys around looking at her. Gretchen seems embarrassed.

"No, no I wouldn't," she says.

I turn to Neil and say, "See, I told you."

Neil hits his head with the palm of his hand and says, "You're killing me."

I have no idea what he's talking about. I am obviously right, and he is clearly wrong.

My writing slowly moves beyond just writing short stories. I now have also amassed a collection of poems and jokes I've written. I occasionally try to write a novel, but I only write a few chapters until I put it aside. I've done this on more than one occasion.

The writing magazine I get in the mail is a constant source of inspiration for me. I learn how famous writers struggled with getting published. Since Neil and I subscribe to the same magazine, we often discuss the articles. I confess to Neil that I probably don't send out my work because I'm afraid of rejection.

We're sitting in Neil's bedroom. He laughs and pulls out a large stack of rejection letters from a drawer in his desk. I'm stunned when Neil tells me he collects them. He then pulls out a much smaller stack of acceptance letters from short story magazines, as well as other literary anthologies, and some other places. Neil shrugs and tells me it's a numbers game.

I'm still not feeling bold enough to send anything out to a publisher. Neil takes out an old edition of a magazine about writing. He starts reading an article about how a rather famous author handled rejection letters. The author knew he wanted to write books for the rest of his life. He got a large piece of plywood and put it in the room where he did his writing. Every time he got a rejection letter, he'd staple it to the plywood board. This author knew that every rejection he received was one step closer to an acceptance. He eventually got his first book accepted, then the next one, and his third book was a huge hit. The story inspires me.

I go home and look through all of my writing. I pick my best short story, go to the latest edition of my writing magazine, look in the markets section, and choose a publisher. I read the requirements several times. I make sure I have the address correct and that the cover letter and short story are typed in the exact way the publisher requires. I include a self-addressed, stamped envelope, get it all together, and head to the post office.

When I get there, I feel nervous. I don't understand my uneasy feeling, but it's like I'm about to expose myself through my writing to a professional editor. My insecurities about not doing well in school, my criminal history, and my family all come flooding into my mind. I have an urge to throw the envelope into the trash and run. I don't. I control myself, get the proper postage, and send my short story to the editor of a magazine.

After leaving the post office, I try to fight off the panic. I ask myself—*what have I just done?* I work on getting calm and try to forget about it. Nothing is going to happen for at least a few weeks. I forget about it, and I get home one day to see a letter from the publisher. I anxiously open it up. It is a form rejection letter. The editor has written on the form rejection letter in pen. He says my story is good, but it has to be even better to get published in his magazine.

I'm so happy. I don't know what to say. An editor at a magazine said my story is good. I easily accept the rejection, but the writing on the rejection letter inspires me. I buy more envelopes, postage, and paper. I get out the current and past issues of my magazines on writing and begin sending out more of my writing to publishers. I don't limit myself to short stories—I send out poems and slogans too. I place some of my writing in the mail each day until my money supply is almost completely depleted.

In time, my stack of rejection letters is larger than Neil's, and I still haven't published anything. I am struggling to fight off depression. I look in the mail one Friday and see two letters from publishers. I put them aside and tell myself I'll look at them later. When I open one letter, a poetry anthology wants to publish one of my poems. They're going to pay me with copies of their anthology with my poem in it and give me $3.00. I am so excited I can't speak. The next letter I open is from a company that wants to buy a slogan I sent them and use it on a button. They're going to pay me $40.00.

I take both of the acceptance letters and tell my parents I'm going to be a published writer. My mother doesn't believe me and ignores the acceptance letters. She advises me to quit making things up. I show my father and he smiles. He then asks how much I would get paid per hour if I had a job with them. I try to explain that's not how it works, and he doesn't seem to understand. He tells me if I can do this, why can't I do better in school? I drop it and ask him about where he's going to be golfing today. He starts to tell me and seems to forget about my publishing success.

I call my friend Neil and tell him. He is very excited for me. Neil offers to take me to lunch to celebrate. During lunch, we talk about writing, writers, and things we are currently working on for publication. Neil is very involved in writing his first science fiction novel. I figure I'll just keep writing short stories. I show Neil some of my humor columns that were inspired by Erma Bombeck and Art Buchwald. He laughs and tells me I'm really funny. It is a great time.

I get the payment from the slogan company and some buttons with my slogan on them. I wear one of the buttons to school. A teacher asks me about the button at the end of class. I say I wrote the slogan. He doesn't believe me. I'm ready for him. I show him the letter from the company accepting my slogan.

He just tosses it down on his desk, smiles, and says, "So, you make money selling slogans to companies and you struggle with my class? I don't understand it."

A kid from the back yells, "He probably stole it."

Other kids in the class laugh as they pass by me to get out of the room. I take my letter from the teacher's desk, put it with my books, and go to my next class.

I anticipated people being impressed with my accomplishment. I thought they would look at me differently. My hope was they would think of me as something other than a thief and a guy from a bad home.

I learned something that day. When people have labeled you in their minds, no matter what you do, they won't let it go. Believing I am something other than a lousy student and a bad kid is difficult for most people. Everyone seems to be more comfortable thinking about my past rather than acknowledging any positive changes I've made in my life. I begin to believe my label will never change no matter what I do. I try to fight back my feelings of anger and frustration, but it's a real struggle.

CHAPTER 23

Adult World Fast Approaching

When school is over this year, I realize I will be seventeen at the end of summer. Next year will be my last year of high school. This is the time when adults begin to tell you that it's important for you to decide what you will do when high school is over. In some families, the only option is going to college. In other families, working in the family business or getting a job in a company where relatives work is their only option. Some kids in my class are going to attend technical school. I am among the confused and clueless kids who have no idea what they would like to do when high school is over. I find thinking about it upsetting.

Before school is out, I meet with a high school guidance counselor. She has my school records and looks at me, back at my records, then looks at me again and smiles.

"Let's start by you telling me what you would like to do after high school," she says.

"I have no idea what I want to do after high school. That's why I'm here, to get some suggestions."

She looks at my school records again and then says, "Well, academics don't seem to be your strength. Do you want to go to college? If so, I would suggest going to a community college. You can then transfer to a four-year program once you finish at the community college."

"I don't like school. I don't think college is for me. What else do you have?"

"You could try and get in a work-study program where you go to a job during some of the day and then come to school the rest of the day?"

"I don't know if there is a job, I would want to do that much to be in such a program."

"You're not giving me much to work with here. Have you thought of the military?"

"My dad was in the military for 26 years. I don't know if that's for me."

"At this point your options are limited. I think you need to think about things and get back to me."

"I'd like to be a writer."

"Okay, you'd need to go to college for that, so we're back to considering community college."

"Well, Ray Bradbury didn't go to college. Neither did Mark Twain or H.G. Wells, William Faulkner, or Truman Capote. None of them went to college, and they're all famous writers."

"Do you know if any of them had a guidance counselor talk to them about college?"

"I don't know."

The guidance counselor lets out a huge sigh.

"And I don't know either. Why don't you do some thinking and come back when you have a better idea of what you want. Then we can start working to make it happen for you. Does that sound fair?"

"Yeah, it sounds fair."

I walk out of the guidance counselor's office and then, for the first time, I feel it. I will be done with high school next year. It will be all over. Then I will have to do something with my life. I'll be free, but also have to find a way to take care of myself. I try not to think about it, but I realize the reality of being an adult is coming toward me at a high speed.

My mother handles the situation of what I should do after my impending high school graduation in her usual way.

"I want you out of this house by the time you're eighteen. There is no reason for you to stay here after that age."

"What if I don't have a job or place to live?"

"Not my problem. Talk to your father."

I go to talk with my father, and he says I should go into the military. That way, I'll have a job, as well as a place to live and food. I try to explain how I want to be a writer. He tells me that's fine, I just have to be able to pay rent with it. I try to explain how it takes time. He doesn't want to hear it. My father recommends I go into the military like my half-sister. I tell him she tried to kill herself when she was in the Army. My father lets me know he doesn't care. He considers it my best option.

I speak to my friend Neil. He got a very good score on his SAT and is looking at different colleges. A few have offered him academic scholarships. He's struggling with which scholarship to accept. Neil lets me know he could never be in the military. My friend Roger is set to start working at the plant where his father and Nate work. I ask him if it's what he wants to do after high school. He shrugs his shoulders and changes the subject. Tim is set to go to an electronics school and become an electronics technician. I feel lost.

I often spend my days walking along the river and other places by myself. I've come to the conclusion that I want to be a writer, but it's not realistic. I have to get a job and make money. I can't stay at my parents' home. My mother can't wait for me to live someplace else. My father can't comprehend anything other than being in the military. I'm scared and confused. I don't know what I'm going to do with my life. It's one more time when I feel my past is controlling my future, and there is nothing I can do about it.

It's summer, and Tim and I are exploring the banks of the river. We're walking farther than we usually do. We both have BB guns and are shooting at things along the way. I have a pistol and Tim has a rifle. I shoot at a shiny piece of metal, and we laugh at the ting sound it makes. Tim shoots at a can on a cement wall and knocks it over. It is a perfect shot. As we walk, we talk about the next school year being our last year in high school.

I say, "I have to tell you, I envy you going to electronics school. I have no idea what I'm going to do when I graduate."

Tim looks at me and chuckles.

He says, "Do you think I want to go to electronics school? Do you think that is something I really want to do?"

"If not, then why are you doing it?"

"I have no idea what I want to do. My dad said I could only stay in his house after high school if I went to school. I didn't want to go to college, I'm like you, I don't like school. There aren't any good jobs for kids just out of high school. I took the test to get into the electronic school and barely passed, but I did pass. My dad is willing to pay for it, so that's why I'm going to electronics school after graduation. It's not something I want to do, it's something I have to do, so I have a place to eat and sleep."

"So, you're going to get up, go to school, come home at the end of the day, and sleep in your bedroom just like in high school. The big difference is now you'll have to drive into the city for school."

"Yeah, that's pretty much it."

We walk along the river in silence for a while. I realize the big difference between me and Tim is that I want change in my life. I want to get away from this town. I want to escape the history I have here and everyone who has given me a label. I figure out I feel trapped, and I want to be free. I want to do something that takes me away from this place.

"You ever plan on leaving this town?"

"Well, I've only lived in one house my entire life. I don't know if I'm ready to change that much. I like things the way they are right now. You plan on leaving?"

"Yeah, I can't stand it here. Do you know there are other places to see and things to explore? Why do you want to limit yourself to just living here?"

"Hey, I know there are other places, but I don't care. I can go on vacations and see other places. I don't have to live there to experience them. I'm fine living right here."

I have no connection with Tim's thinking. It seems so foreign to me. I then remember reading in a book that if everything you love and care about is in one location, you tend to not want to go beyond that location. I think I understand why Tim may not want things in his life to change. I have nothing I love or care about in this town. I don't understand Tim, and I'm sure I seem pretty odd to him. I decide to keep my thoughts to myself.

A few days later I'm at Neil's house. I'm still confused about what to do when I graduate high school. I ask Neil if he's looking forward to going to college.

Neil says, "You mean am I looking forward to doing classwork, projects, taking tests, and more? The answer would be no. If you are asking if I'm looking forward to living away from home, making new friends, and being a wild college kid? The answer would be a strong yes."

"I thought you liked school," I say.

Neil smiles.

"You are like my family. Everybody thinks because I'm good at school, I like it. I hate it. It's easy for me. In my family, you either get good grades or face the wrath of your parents and other family members. Grades are everything. I've had to be a good student to survive in my house. I didn't have much of an option,"

"Don't you have an academic scholarship to a college?"

"Ah, not a college, a university. I've been offered more than one and I have not decided which one I will be accepting. I should say, my parents and other family members haven't decided which scholarship I will accept. It's not really up to me right now. My parents have chosen the classes I've taken in high school since my freshman year. They have figured out my life for me."

"Don't you feel trapped?"

"Oh, it sucks, but what am I going to do? If I go against my parents, they have a meltdown. I write and publish things, but I don't dare show them. My father would be furious if I did something like that without letting him see what I wrote or having input into where I sent it. My writing is a big secret I keep from everyone.

I told my parents I wanted to be an entomologist, and they were upset. According to them, I can be a lawyer like my father, a CPA like my grandfather, or a physician like my sister. So, that is one thing I get to decide for my life."

I look at Neil and feel so sorry for him. I realize my parents' lack of involvement in my life has provided me so much freedom. They don't care about what happens in my life, but they aren't trying to control it either. I can do whatever I want, and as long as I'm out of their house by the time I'm eighteen, I don't think they'd care what I end up doing. I'm also not emotionally attached to anyone or anything in this town. I leave Neil's house feeling good about my level of freedom.

I decide to go to Roger's house on a Saturday. I haven't talked to him for a long time. When I get there, I see him and Nate working on something in their garage.

I yell, "Hello, long time no see, what's up with you guys?"

Nate and Roger stop what they're doing. As is their tradition, I'm asked to go around back and get some beer. They've now got a place cleaned out with chairs so people can sit in a circle and drink. It looks nice. We all sit down on chairs and open cans of beer.

"What brings you here, stranger?" asks Nate.

I say, "Hey, I was around and thought I'd stop by to see if you guys were here. How goes work at the plant?"

"Ah, you know, it sucks, but I'm making good money and I get to see my dad, uncle, and other relatives during the day. So, it's not too bad."

I look at Roger and say, "You looking forward to joining your family at the plant?"

Roger looks sad and says, "I don't have a choice."

Nate interrupts and says, "Ah, don't be upset, little brother. You'll be working in a place where our grandfather worked for over forty years. Think of it as a family tradition."

"What would you rather do?" I say to Roger.

"Play in a band. I'd like to go to New York or Los Angeles and get with other musicians and get a band together. That is what I would like to do," says Roger.

"Dream on, little brother. You aren't as good on the drums as you believe. It'd be a disaster. Then mom and dad would have to pay to bring you back here. I bet you'd then have to work at the plant to pay the money you'd owe mom and dad. It's best you put in your time at the plant like everybody else. Quit thinking you're better than the rest of us," says Nate.

Nate and Roger start arguing. I've never seen them fight like this before. I sense Nate wanted to go to a city and form a band when he graduated high school, but gave up and worked at the plant. Now Roger is thinking about pursuing Nate's dream. It is as if Nate is trying to make Roger as miserable as he is by his little brother working at the plant. Even in this family, I guess misery loves company. I finish my beer and tell them I have to leave. Roger and Nate seem upset that I'm going. They start blaming one another for me leaving. I can't get away from them fast enough.

As I'm on my way home, I think about my friends. I talk to some more of them and hear the same stories. All of them are making choices for their life based on what their family tells them. Some feel trapped, others have decided to just give in and some don't want the routine of school and home to end. I don't know what I'm going to decide. I've always been different from other kids in town, and I now realize that might just be a good thing.

CHAPTER 24

A New Attitude

I'm five years old. I get out of bed and I'm looking forward to being at kindergarten. After getting dressed like I do every day, I go into the kitchen. My mother isn't there. I look inside her bedroom, and she is sleeping. I get my small box of cereal. The container of milk is too big for me, so I eat it dry. I get a jar of peanut butter and a piece of bread. I'm not good at spreading peanut butter on bread, so I take my finger, put peanut butter on it, and spread it on the bread. It works just fine. I put the peanut butter back and my mother comes into the kitchen. Her hair is a mess, there are bags under her eyes, and her voice is raspy.

"What are you doing?" she asks.

"I got breakfast and dressed like a big boy," I respond.

"Ah, go brush your teeth,"

"Okay."

I'm happy and skip into the bathroom. I brush my teeth and spit a little too much, but I wipe my face with a towel. I look at myself in the mirror—I think I'm ready for kindergarten. I go back out to the kitchen. My mother has her head down and is smoking a cigarette.

"You have to walk to school by yourself today. I don't feel well. You know the way."

"I want someone to be with me," I protest.

My mother ignores me. She opens the door and tells me to go. I'm scared. She tells me to quit being a baby. I'm given a little shove out the door, and I'm suddenly standing outside. I don't know what to do as I watch the front door close. I start walking. When I get to the intersection with the traffic light, I'm too scared to cross. I wait until people come up to the light. I cross the street with them. I walk up another block and down one more block. I again wait for people to cross the street with the traffic light. After getting across with them, I can then walk to school. I no longer have to deal with any more intersections. I get to school and the other kids have their parents walking by and letting them join the other kids on the playground. I go and play with the other kids until kindergarten starts. When school is over, we can't leave until a parent comes to get us. I don't know what to do. I walk behind a friend and their parents as they leave. It seems as if they're taking me home.

I make it home. I go to open the front door and it's locked. I'm upset and feel like crying. I sit down on the ground near the front door. I don't know how long I am there, but my half-sister shows up. She has a key to the front door, and we go inside. My mother wakes up from her sleep. She comes out, sits at the kitchen table, and lights a cigarette. My half-sister asks me who walked me to school. I tell her I went by myself. My half-sister looks at my mother who says she doesn't know what I'm talking about. My half-sister tells me I'm a little liar and walks away. I don't understand what a little liar is, but I think I've been a good boy. I tell my mother I did go to school by myself. I'm a big boy. She looks away from me and I'm confused. I go and turn on the television. My favorite cartoons will be on soon.

When I return to high school for my senior year, I have a new attitude. I no longer feel that I'm less than the other kids in my class. Most of them appear to me to be children who have their parents running their lives. Many of the other kids who have a bad past and horrible home lives haven't made it this far. Some are in juvenile hall, others quit school, and some have moved away. I'm one of the few who is a senior.

I now lack a fear of others judging me for my past. I honestly don't care what they think of me. This has resulted in having enough courage to try out for a school play my senior year. Our school will be putting on a production of the musical *South Pacific*. I have no idea why I did it. Signing up for the auditions was an impulse move. I'd never previously been part of a school play. This will be all very new to me.

On the day of the auditions, I realize several kids are there who have previously been part of many school plays. I see a girl singing a song as part of her audition, and I'm impressed. I overhear other kids talking about all the plays they have been in previously with theater companies. My mind tells me the chances of me getting picked to be part of the musical are between slim and none. I've recently read in a writing magazine that writers often do things for the experience. This is how they know what it feels like to do something before they write about it. I believe this experience will let me know what it feels like to audition for a high school musical.

I'm given a script and told to study it. My character is an Army officer who yells at some people in a particular scene. It seems to me this character is someone I understand. When it's my turn, the teacher, who is the director, asks me a few questions about my previous experience with plays. I'm honest and realize he's not impressed with my answers. He is going to read the part of an obnoxious sailor, and I will read the part of the Army officer who does the yelling. When he reads his lines, I can feel the officer's anger. I start yelling my lines like I'm angry, I walk up to the teacher and point my finger at him and finish my lines. After I'm done, the teacher just looks at me for a few seconds.

He then starts writing on his clipboard and says, "Well, that was believable. Thank you for your time."

The teacher motions for the next person to come up and read some lines. I leave the audition feeling pretty good. I don't think I'll get picked to be in the musical, but I tell myself it was good to have the experience. I write about it that night.

A few days later, the results of the audition are posted near the school auditorium. I don't know if I want to look, since I'm certain I didn't get picked. I figure I should at least take a glance. I'm shocked to see my name on the list of kids who were chosen to be in the musical. I look at it, and then I look at it again. I don't believe it. Kids are trying to get around me to get a better look at the list. I stand there in shock. I'm going to be in our high school production of *South Pacific*. All I had to do was yell and scream at someone. I think I may have trained my whole life for this particular role.

I go to the first cast meeting, and we are each given a script with our names on it. Our lines and scenes are highlighted. I will be playing a sailor in some scenes and an Army officer in others. As a sailor, I sing with the other guys, and as an Army officer, I get to yell at people. I don't know about singing, but I am a natural when it comes to yelling at people.

There are a few jocks who will be in the play. None of the greasers. The rest of the cast are nerds and unclassified students such as myself. When I tell my mother I will be in the musical, she says that is good. She is too involved in watching a movie and wants me to tell her more when the commercials come on. I tell my father, and he wants to know how much it will cost him. I let him know I can pay for it. He then says okay, lifts his newspaper, and goes back to reading.

I meet a new type of kid who is involved in the production. These kids are creative and most of them like art, reading, and stories. I fit in with most of them. I make a new friend named Jay. He is as unclassified of a student as me. He was a jock in his younger days, but he only did it to please his father. He isn't a good student except for math. Jay also has no idea what he is going to do when our class graduates. He tells me about his lousy home life one day, and we quickly become good friends.

Each night I forgo my time for writing. I focus on memorizing my lines. When I go to rehearsal, I soon learn that putting together the production of a play is a long and involved process. We have to learn scene changes, where to stand, what has to happen when we say our lines. I work on slowing down when I deliver my lines. There are things we must do between scene changes. We enter and exit at certain places. I soon realize learning my lines is only a small part of being in the musical.

The director yells at kids, and even throws props when he's upset. I get angry and ask one of the kids near me if we need to say something. He just laughs. I'm told the director does this every production. This is an effective way for kids to remember to do things correctly. One guy says he tried being nice during his first play, and it turned out to be a huge mess. The kids in the cast didn't take him seriously, forgot their lines, and it was a disaster. When he started yelling, everyone remembered what they needed to do. It doesn't seem to upset any of the kids in the production. They find it funny. I feel better after speaking with them.

After rehearsing for weeks, we get close to the production date. I volunteer with some other kids in the musical to go and get the costumes. We are all loaded onto a school van and then make the trip to a costume shop in the city. Once the van is filled with costumes, a few of us agree to sit in the back to make certain nothing falls and breaks. Jay is with us and is sitting next to the back doors of the van.

It's a cold day, so we are all wearing our winter coats. The roads are in terrible condition. We hit a bump, the back doors fly open, and Jay falls out. We are all in shock as we watch him hit the road on his back and slide. A car right behind us slams on his brakes and avoids hitting Jay. I start screaming for the teacher to stop the van. The girls don't move and seem like they can't speak. Then the most amazing thing happens. I think Jay is dead, but he gets up and starts running down the road, chasing the van. He is running faster than most people on the track team. I then see the most amazing thing happen. Jay catches up to the van and hops inside. The teacher finally pulls over. We explain to him what happened. The teacher makes certain Jay and the rest of us are all okay. He then closes the van's back doors and locks them. Jay doesn't have even a scratch. The back of his winter coat is torn to shreds, but he's okay. I asked him where he learned to run so fast. Jay tells me he has no idea. I suggest he may be able to get a track scholarship for college. We all laugh.

The production slowly evolves from learning lines to learning when to enter and exit and then how to handle each scene. By the time we get the costumes, we all pretty well know what we should do during the musical. Then there is a dress rehearsal. We have to work on our knowledge of where to go with changing costumes. This takes a while, but we all master it.

Then we have a rehearsal with full costumes and make-up. I don't want to wear make-up. I'm told it's just stage make-up, so I show up better under the lights. I also get no sympathy from some girls who think I'm a baby. They tell me how they have to put on make-up every day. If I mention a girl who doesn't wear make-up, they whisper that the girl should wear make-up.

I'm enjoying being part of the musical. My favorite part is a scene I get with Sonya, the girl who laughed at me when I asked her on a date. During one scene, we have to walk arm-in-arm onto the stage and greet everyone at a party.

As we're waiting to go out on stage, I don't look at Sonya but say, "I'm going to tell everyone in school I touched you."

To my surprise, she smiles and says, "Stop it, be nice, we're in a show."

The next time we rehearse the scene I say, "Why don't we go somewhere and make out, so we can feel like a real couple. We could do it for the sake of the show."

She laughs and says, "You are bad. You need to behave."

Another time I walk on stage arm-in-arm with Sonya and instead of saying my line, I say, "Maybe later I'll try to corral this fine filly I have brought with me to the party."

Others around me laugh as well as Sonya. The director yells, and I do the line correctly the next time. I've never felt so confident around females. I'm not scared of them anymore.

On the first night of the musical, everything goes well. Everyone is a little nervous, but everything goes as planned. During the final night, there is a bowl of highly spiked punch in the guy's dressing room. I see a guy go into the girl's dressing room, and I don't want to know what is happening. I yell at a sailor as an Army officer so well, some people applaud. After I deliver my line when Sonya and I walk into the party during the play, I whisper to Sonya that being a fine filly is one of her special gifts. I say it so only she can hear. Sonya ignores me.

My parents are there the closing night. My mother's oldest daughter is with them. I'm shocked. They come out when it's over and talk to me like all the other family members of the cast. It feels strange. I don't know what to think. They're nice to me, and I decide to be happy about it.

Jay drives an old car his parents had years ago but still works pretty well. He gives me a lift to the cast party. Everyone has had a sufficient amount of alcohol. Sonya makes it a point to introduce me to her boyfriend. I've seen him before and know he is a very nice guy.

I look at him and say, "I understand that Sonya loves it when you call her a fine filly. Is that true?"

Sonya laughs, hits me on the shoulder, and says, "You never stop. You really are bad."

Her boyfriend laughs and says, "I didn't know you liked being called a fine filly, but if you want me to be my fine filly, consider it done."

Sonya hits him on the shoulder and starts to move her boyfriend to another part of the room. She leans back and tells me she hates me, and I laugh. It feels good to be the one who is now laughing at her.

At the end of the night, Jay is driving me home.

"You make any plans for after graduation yet?" I ask.

Jay shrugs his shoulders.

"Nope, how about you?" he says.

"Nothing yet," I respond.

"You know what I'm thinking?

"What?"

"To not have anything planned and see what happens,"

"Might not be a good way to handle things."

"I agree, but that's my plan as of right now."

Jay and I then talk about how much fun it was to be part of the play. When I'm dropped off at my house, I am tired. It's been a long day. I've had a little too much to drink. I'm glad to know someone like Jay who is as confused about what to do in the future as I am. It makes me feel like I'm not alone.

CHAPTER 25

The Writing Life

I'm writing stories in the evenings and sending them out to magazines when I have the money. I'm receiving a lot of form rejection letters. The frustration is building in me. I read other stories that have been published in these magazines, and I believe my stories are much better. My friend Neil agrees to read a few of my stories. It appears the problem is not with the story; it is with my spelling, punctuation, and grammar. I've never been a good student and only did what must be done to not fail a class. Now, that attitude from the past has come back to impact my life.

Neil likes my stories a lot and edits a few, but I know I can't depend on him for all my editing. He has a lot of things going on in his life. I get a book from the local library and study grammar. I get a dictionary and begin to carefully edit my stories before I send them out. My publishing success is small, but it is quite important to me.

I've developed a sense of confidence after being selected to be in the high school play, and I decide to further test my abilities. I see a sign for anyone who wants to be part of the high school newspaper. As the day of the try-out approaches, I experience a wave of insecurity. I have to fight off the feelings of not being as smart or as good of a student as the other kids. If someone knows about my past with the law and mentions it, I know I'll be extremely upset.

I'm dealing with my internal conflicts as I walk into the room where the auditions are being given. I'm there at the last minute. I start feeling intimidated as I'm surrounded by some of the smartest kids in the school. Neil is sitting beside me. I know some of the kids who are in the musical are here, including Jay. Kids who have been with the newspaper in previous years give a talk. The teacher in charge then finishes up by discussing all of the things involved with being on the high school newspaper. The teacher explains how we will need to gather information and produce an article in a specified amount of time. We are all given a writing assignment. There are other papers attached to the writing assignment that is research for our particular story. I don't remember when I've been this nervous.

I take a deep breath and go into my writing world. This is not like when I'm home and can take as much time as I like to write something. We're given only a certain amount of time to finish the writing assignment.

When I finish, I believe what I've written is just average. I know if given enough time, I could make it much better. I carefully check the grammar, spelling, and punctuation before the time is over and our stories are collected. In my mind, this did not go well. What I believe I have provided is a piece of writing that is only average and needs to be properly edited.

I then go about my daily routine at school and home. The idea of being on the school newspaper begins to fade from my thoughts. In my mind, the story I wrote and handed in wasn't all that great. I keep telling myself it was a nice try by me.

I had completely forgotten about it until I see Neil at lunch one day. He comes over and tells me congratulations are in order.

"What are you talking about?" I ask.

Neil smiles and says, "I'm talking about you. You're on the school newspaper. They posted the list of names of students who will be on the school newspaper. I saw your name. I'm also going to be part of it this year. My parents will be furious, but I don't care."

"No."

"Oh, yes, my parents are going to see this as something taking away from my academic studies. They're going to be quite upset."

"No, I mean, you actually saw my name?"

"Unless you've recently changed it. Yes, I saw your name. You are on the school newspaper. Good thing I told you. We have a meeting after school tomorrow. You need to start remembering things. I don't mind being your editor, but I draw the line at being your secretary."

I smile and say, "Thanks, I'm going to go look at the list."

"Okay, but trust me, your name is there."

I make my way out of the cafeteria and up the steps to the room where the high school newspaper is produced. On the list outside I recognize my name. It's there for all the world to see. I also see Neil's and Jay's names on the list. I don't know what to say. I feel as if there has been a mistake. I go into the room and see the teacher who runs the school newspaper. She is by herself working at her desk. Her name is Miss Winnis.

I knock on the door and walk into the room.

She smiles and says, "I see it is one of my future reporters. What can I do for you?"

"Ah, I don't know how to say this, but are you sure my story was okay?" I ask.

She opens a folder on her desk, goes through all sorts of papers, and then pulls out my story.

"Yes, you wrote a very good story. You covered all the major points within the allotted time. Your grammar and punctuation were fine. Yes, I want you to be on the school newspaper. Is there a problem?"

"No, I'm very excited about it. I just didn't think my story was all that great, and I'm surprised. I mean I don't do that well in school."

Miss Winnis chuckles and puts my story back in the folder. She then puts the folder back to its original spot on her desk.

"Well, don't be too surprised. What you do in other classes doesn't matter to me. I only look at your writing. Over thirty kids tried out for the school newspaper, and I only picked twelve. You're one of them. I hope you can make it to the meeting after school tomorrow. If you have any more questions, you can ask them then. Is that okay?"

"Yes, yes, that's great."

Leaving the room, I feel a special type of happiness. I have a sense that the terrible things in my past are losing their control over me. The freedom I'm experiencing goes deep within me.

I go to the meeting after school. We learn how the paper is put together, how it is distributed, and more. We're given our first assignments and the date they need to be given to the school newspaper's editor. I'm excited, but a little nervous.

The first few articles go well and I'm getting comfortable writing for the newspaper. I have a fun experience one day when the newspaper is completed and we all have some free time. There is nothing for us to do before we begin working on the next edition. I've recently been reading books by Erma Bombeck and Art Buchwald. They inspire me to write a few humor columns about school life. I type them up and put them on my desk. Then, I leave for the next class without realizing I had left them on the desk.

The next day, Miss Winnis and the high school newspaper's editor want to see me. I instantly feel they've discovered my criminal past, and I'll be thrown off the high school newspaper. I resign myself to having had a good time, but a person with my past doesn't get to be on something like the high school newspaper.

The three of us go into an empty room and I'm asked to sit down. The name of the high school newspaper's editor is Janis. She takes out some papers and hands them to me.

"Did you write this?" asks Janis.

I suddenly realize they're the humor columns I must have forgotten on my desk.

"Well, yeah, I wrote them, I didn't mean for anybody to see them. Is that what this is all about? We can just throw them away. I've always gotten all my story assignments done and turned in before their due date like you've asked. I didn't mean to upset anyone. I'm sorry," I say.

Janis and Miss Winnis look at one another and smile.

"We're not upset by these humor columns. We're impressed by them. Not everyone has the talent to write something like this," says Miss Winnis.

Janis then says, "What we want to know is if you can write one of these humor columns for each of the remaining issues of the school paper. I have to admit, when I read them, I laughed out loud. You are very funny."

I struggle to speak and say, "Yeah, sure, ah, no problem."

"So, we have a deal? You'll write one of these humor columns for each of the remaining issues of the high school newspaper?" says Miss Winnis.

I want to say many things but my ability to speak has momentarily escaped me. I look at Miss Winnis, Janis, and then at my humor columns.

"You guys are serious about this, aren't you?"

"I just need to know if you can do what we're asking," says Jannis. I smile.

"Yes, writing these humor columns comes easy to me. It's the easiest type of writing I've ever done. It won't be any problem for me to write one for each of the remaining issues of the high school newspaper. Sure, I'll do it."

Janis wants to use two of the humor columns they found on my desk, and then I will need to write some more. After leaving that meeting, I go to my next class. I can't focus on history, the only thing I'm thinking about are ideas I have for my humor column in the high school newspaper.

I do my usual assignments for the high school newspaper. I write about the girl's junior varsity basketball game, a Spanish club party, as well as a student who received a full academic scholarship to an Ivy League university. There is also a student who won a dancing competition in another state. I find these articles interesting to write, but my heart is with my humor columns. I easily write more than the newspaper can print. I tell Miss Winnis and Janis I just want to give them a variety to choose from for each edition.

The lesson of writing humor to be read by people without any sense of humor is something I learn quickly. In one humor column, I write about the association between different characters from scary movies and the types of people who teach certain classes. I write how Godzilla strikes me as a gym teacher. King Kong is part of the administration. The invisible man could have been a guidance counselor. The 50-foot woman would be the coach for the girl's basketball team and more. Everyone working at the high school newspaper thinks the column is rather funny. I believed it would be met with enthusiastic laughter from all over the school. I soon learn I am wrong.

On my way to gym class, some kids gave me a thumbs up about the humor column. I hear people tell me it is funny. Others tell me I shouldn't have made fun of the gym teacher. I didn't mention his name; I said a high school gym teacher. When I arrive at gym class, I realize my humor didn't sit well with someone as egocentric as our gym teacher.

He walks up to me and says, "So, you think I look like Godzilla?"

I smile and say, "If you're referring to my humor column, I didn't mention any names. I made a general reference to gym teachers. It was talking about any gym teacher. So, let me ask you, do you think you look like Godzilla? If so, I would have to disagree."

After I'm done speaking, I realize I've become a nerd. A nerd with bad grades, but I have a nerd attitude.

The gym teacher gets close to me and says in my ear, "Listen up, you little smart-mouthed asshole. What do you think I am? You want to say something to me, you say it to my face and don't write it in that piece of shit high school newspaper like a coward. Do you understand me?"

"You do think the world revolves around you, don't you?"

The gym teacher blows his whistle and points to the lockers. He tells me I get a zero for the day because of my attitude. He tells the rest of the class he is not going to put up with a smart ass like me in his class.

It doesn't bother me. I've taken enough gym classes that if I get a zero until the end of the school year, I'll still get a passing grade for the class. I'm not going to college or going to become an athlete, so I'm not worried.

It's the same experience with every humor column I write. Most people think they're very funny. Others find a way to be offended by them. I am learning about the power of the written word.

Jay calls me one day and wants to know if I'd like to go and hang out at the mall. I agree. We go and walk, look at stores, and make an attempt to speak to some pretty girls. Looking at all the things we want, Jay and I realize how much money we don't have. It's a typical trip to the mall.

As we're sitting Jay says, "You decided what you're going to do after graduation?"

"Not yet, I have no idea what I'm going to do," I say.

"My parents are putting some pressure on me to do something. I'm kind of scared. I don't want to go to college. All the jobs around here are crap. I would never pass the test to get into a technical school. I don't even want to go to community college."

"Yeah, I agree. It's like I know I have to do something, but I just can't decide. All my options seem to suck."

"Hey, maybe something will come along that will take away our troubles and help us figure out something to do after high school."

"Yeah, and I'm getting an idea for another humor column."

The two of us sit there finishing our sodas and feel sad and upset.

CHAPTER 26

Anchors Aweigh

I'm in my bedroom working on some stories. It's a long three-day weekend. My only plans are to do homework, write stories, and watch television. The phone rings and I hear my mother yell that it's for me. When I pick up the receiver, it's my friend Jay.

"Guess what?" says Jay.

I laugh and say, "You got a date with Marie Tibbins?"

"I wish. Hey, a Navy recruiter called me. He asked if I'd like to go and take the test to get in the Navy. He said there is no obligation to take the test, and they'll provide breakfast and lunch. It's at the federal building in the city. He said I could take someone with me if I wanted. I thought you might like to go."

I have trouble mentally processing anything other than free breakfast, lunch, and a day in the city. It sounds like a good time. I agree to go with Jay.

The next day, the recruiter picks me up in his car. Jay is sitting in the front passenger seat. I'm in the back next to a kid who is wearing thick glasses, has acne, and looks like he's facing a firing squad. His name is Albert. I soon learn he doesn't want to go into the Navy, but his parents demand it of him.

As we drive to the city, I soon realize they expect me to take the test to get into the Navy.

I get the recruiter's attention and say, "Ah, I hope I'm not expected to take the test. I'm just here to help my friend Jay."

This Navy recruiter is someone who could have sold a person a car they already owned. He launches into a speech and I soon I soon hear a speech that results in me taking the test. I realize he's good.

"Oh, come on now, it's just a test, you take them all the time in school. You don't have to join the Navy because you take a test. Besides, if you don't want to take the test, I can't pay for your breakfast or lunch," says the recruiter.

The thought of not being able to have free food shocks me. I then figure it's just a test. He's right, I take them all the time in school when there is no free food involved. This should be easy. If I don't do well on the test, I won't be able to join the Navy, but I will still have had a free breakfast and lunch. I figure this is a good deal.

Once we arrive at the federal building, we go into a cafeteria. Jay, Albert, and I all have a rather filling breakfast. There are eggs, potatoes, toast, bacon, sausage, orange juice, coffee, tea, pancakes, and more. It's great. We then go up to the testing room. It's like a room in school and consists of old wooden chairs that have a flat area to put the tests. It takes hours. The test is called the Armed Services Vocational Aptitude Battery (ASVAB) test. They are all multiple-choice questions. I don't find it too difficult. It takes a few hours to complete the test. When it's over, I'm glad.

We then get to go to the cafeteria and have a rather large lunch. There are hamburgers, hot dogs, french fries, salads, fruit, sodas, iced tea, chocolate cake, and candies for dessert. I never knew simply taking a test for the military could result in you being fed so well.

On my way home, I figure that's the end of it. I had my day and enjoyed myself. Jay is excited about the possibility of being in the Navy. He has a pamphlet the recruiter gave him about being in the Navy, and he's talking about how he'd look in different uniforms. Jay talks about what ships he'd like to be on and all the foreign countries he plans to visit. When the recruiter asks me what I think, I tell him I wish the school fed us this well when we take our tests. I try to be polite and tell him I need time to think about it. When I get dropped off at my house, I realize I never told my parents where I was going for the day.

I tell my father I took the test to be in the Navy, and he seems confused.

"Why would you want to be in the Navy?"

"I never said I wanted to be in the Navy. I took the test and got free food."

"Why would you want to spend all that time on the ocean in those boats?"

Now I'm angry and say, "Because I want to travel the world and see lots of foreign countries."

"You should go into the Air Force. That's the best place to serve."

"What if I don't want to join the Air Force? What if I want to be on a ship at sea?"

He then laughs and says some rather derogatory things about sailors. My father was in the Army during World War II. When the Air Force became its own branch of the military in 1947, he opted to join the Air Force. I got so sick and tired growing up and hearing about his exploits in the Air Force.

When I tell my mother, she shrugs her shoulders. She starts talking about how her daughter had to join the Army after she graduated from high school, and it was my father's fault. Her son joined the Marines right out of high school, went to Vietnam, and got wounded, all because of my father. My mother believes it is only fair that I should be in the military right after graduating from high school. She tells me I'm no better than her children. She doubts I'd make it in the Army or the Marines. I leave before my anger gets the best of me.

A day or two later, I pick up the pamphlet the Navy recruiter handed me as I left his car. I read about visiting other countries as well as getting training and experience. I then realize I'd be away from this town. My past would stay here, and I would be away from it. Nobody would know anything about me in the Navy. I would be judged on how I am now rather than my past and my family's history. Joining the Navy starts to look more attractive to me.

The next week I get a call from the Navy recruiter. He tells me I scored very high on the ASVAB test. I qualify to do just about any job the Navy has to offer. I'm then informed Jay is going down on Saturday to take the physical and wants to know if I'd like to join him. I want to confirm that I'll be getting breakfast and lunch. Once I'm told yes, it's a deal.

I speak with Jay and learn he also did very well on the test. He wants to be an air traffic controller. When Jay asks me what I want to do, I have no idea. I'm still not sure I'll join the Navy. I keep thinking about all the adventures famous writers had while in the military. Ernest Hemingway, J.D. Salinger, Kurt Vonnegut, and other famous writers served in the military. I think it could be an experience that may result in the creation of many more stories from me.

On the day of the physical exam, the breakfast is as good as it was before. The recruiter sits with me and asks about what type of work I want to do in the Navy. I tell him I want to be a writer. He tells me I did qualify to be a journalist in the Navy if I want. I'm excited. Then he tells me they seldom go to sea; they usually stay on land during the majority of their enlistment. He tells me I need to think about it if I want to travel. I'm instantly conflicted.

The one thing I learn on the day I get the physical is that there is a long line for everything in the military. There are also many forms that need to be completed. They have a form for everything. I'm talking to one person who is processing paperwork.

I ask him, "Is there a form you have to fill out so you can order more forms?

He gives me a strange look and says, "Of course, how else would you get more forms?"

"Is there a form you have to fill out to get the form that has to be completed to get the form requesting more forms?"

He just looks at me like I'm crazy and says, "Whatever."

Things are set up in stations. You have a form that has to be signed off from each station. I get a chest x-ray, my height and weight are measured, my eyes are examined, I give various samples for testing, and more. My ears are checked, the joints in my legs and arms are checked, my throat is checked. As I go through each station, I keep telling myself they'll eventually run out of things to check.

When I go to lunch, it's as grand as it was before, but these free meals seem to be less important to me. Jay tells me about some guys he's met from other schools. It seems he didn't realize it, but a cousin of his is here getting a physical to join the Air Force. He was surprised to see him. Jay tells me how the recruiter has fixed it so he can go to air traffic controller school in the Navy as soon as he completes basic training. He's extremely excited. I'm glad for him, but I don't even know if I'm going to join the Navy.

The Navy recruiter comes over to me and has someone with him. I'm introduced to a man who worked as a journalist in the Navy for ten years but is now a recruiter. The man's name is Brian. He sits down across from me and says he understands I'd like to be a journalist in the Navy. Brian is a very nice guy. He answers all of my questions. I learn how it is similar to writing for the high school newspaper. You're given assignments to cover stories happening on the local base and elsewhere in the Navy. He did confirm he spent most of his time on base and only spent a short amount of time on an aircraft carrier. I'm glad he took the time to speak with me. I sense the recruiter is doing everything in his power to answer my questions. I'm also being well-fed.

In the afternoon, I have an experience that I have never had happen to me before. I'm one of thirty guys who are told to remove all of their clothes. I'm completely embarrassed. The need to deal with being around other naked guys hasn't happened since I played football. During that time, I just hid my face, got changed, and left. The thought of simply leaving crosses my mind. I don't want to do this. It seems as if I may be the only one who has a problem with it. Most guys have all of their clothes off and are lined up like we were told. I struggle and refuse to look anywhere but straight ahead.

Standing naked in line with dozens of other guys is very awkward for me. I'm counting the seconds until this is over. The next thing I know, a man dressed in a white coat and referred to as the doctor comes into the room. He is smoking a pipe and is going to each of the guys, standing in front of them for a few seconds, asking questions followed by a few seconds of silence, and he then moves on to the next guy.

When it's my turn, the doctor asks me about strains and anything damaging my groin area. His pipe smoke is getting in my eyes and I cough. He then tells me to cough and touches my privates. With his pipe smoke going into my face, coughing isn't a problem. If he wasn't a doctor, I would have become violent. After the doctor is done with you, it's okay to get dressed.

I have a feeling of being violated. I feel sorry for his wife. I can't imagine what will happen when she asks this doctor what he did today at work.

After dressing and getting in the next line, I ask a guy what that was all about.

He tells me, "They have to check to see if any of us have a hernia."

I say, "I wonder why they just don't ask you."

"Because some of the dumbest assholes in the world try to get into the military. They may not know they have a hernia, or they lie about it. This way they know for certain you don't have one."

All I know for certain is after being checked for a hernia, I want to go home and take a nice hot shower.

I'm very conflicted about joining the Navy. I'd heard stories about being in the military since I was small. My father would tell me about his time of being in the Army and Air Force. When he stopped, my mother would tell me about her son being in the military, her oldest daughter's first husband being in the military. I got so tired of hearing about it.

I don't like the idea of wearing a uniform, marching, and dealing with all the discipline that goes with life in the military. The reality of my situation is that my prospects of what to do after I graduate high school are none. I just don't like school and don't have good grades. I don't know how to do anything for a job. I don't want to work in any of the local manufacturing plants or stores.

My decision comes down to what I want to do after graduation. I know I want to get as far away from this town and my history. I would love to travel and see different countries. The idea of getting paid as it happens seems attractive. I know I could write so many stories. As I think about it, my decision starts to become easier.

CHAPTER 27

Swan Song

I'm six years old and at an amusement park. My father has taken me to the area of the park where the big-kid rides are located. It's just me and him as we stroll around the park. There is a huge roller coaster making loud sounds, and I hear people screaming.

My dad says, "Hey, would you like to go on the big-kid roller coaster?"

"I'm too small," I say.

My dad says, "Don't worry about it, I'll get you on."

We go and stand in line. I look at the roller coaster and when I realize how big it is and how fast it goes, I start to get scared.

"I don't think I want to do this," I say.

Smiling, my dad says, "Ah, come on, it's time for you to be a man. It's just a roller coaster, I won't let anything happen to you."

The closer we get, the more frightened I become. You must be a certain height to get on the ride. The man letting people on the ride knows my father. I'm too small, and so I'm told to stand on the tips of my toes. I'm still just a little too short, but my father's friend winks at my dad and nods to the roller coaster car. We get in, and I'm very scared. My dad is a little angry and tells me to quit being a baby. I need to be a man about this.

There are older kids in front of us who seem so excited. We begin the ride and there is one small dip, but I'm okay. Then we come around a bend real fast and start going slowly up a steep incline. I'm trying to control my fear as we make our way to the top.

I tell my father I don't want to do this. He laughs and tells me it's too late now. We stop once we reach the top. My dad has his arm in front of me and I'm holding it as tightly as possible. I'm trying to not cry. I don't want to be a baby for my dad.

We go down the hill so fast, I close my eyes. We then go fast around the track and up another hill. After this, we do some quick up and down movements. There are some very sharp turns and then the roller coaster car comes to the platform and stops.

My father looks at me and says, "See, there was nothing to be frightened about, now was there?"

I don't want to talk to my father right now. Walking is a struggle for me at first because my knees are shaking. I'm also fighting off the feeling of nausea. I now know I'm not a baby. I'm a man like my father told me to be. I believe I just made him proud.

I'm standing on the porch. My father is sitting on his chair with a newspaper on his lap.

"Why would you want to go out on that boat all the time? It doesn't make any sense. Why don't you join the Air Force? It'd be the best thing for you," he says.

I want to scream. I want to say I don't want to join the Air Force because he was in it, and I'm tired of hearing about it. I don't want to join the Marines because when my mother tells me all the stories about her son being in Vietnam and getting wounded, I want to scream. The thought of joining the Army makes me want to hit things. I'm so tired of hearing how my half-sister had to join the Army because of my father. In the back of my mind, I know these are bad reasons not to join a particular branch of the military, but right now they are my reasons.

"You don't know anything about being in the Navy," I say.

"I know you got to spend all sorts of time on a boat on the sea. During World War II my unit was on some of the Navy's troop transport boats. I said I'd never go back on one of those again even if my life depended on it."

"There are so many different types of ships in the Navy. It's more than just troop transports."

My father looks away and puts his paper up.

I then hear him say, "Do what you want. I don't care."

I'm angry and go into our house. My mother wants to know what is wrong with me. I tell her I'm tired of her and my father acting like the Navy is something horrible. I say it has a lot of opportunities for a guy like me. My mother says she doesn't care what I do, but I have to do something because I can't live with them after I turn eighteen. I want to start breaking things when she tells me I've had it too easy. My mother claims I'd never make it in the Marines or the Army like her kids. She is surprised I passed the test to get into the military. I realize I have absolutely nothing in this house or this town holding me here. I want to leave more than anything.

I get the Navy recruiter's phone number and call him. I've decided to become a sailor. He is excited. It seems my friend Jay is also going to join the Navy. He tells me it's possible for Jay and me to go through basic training together if I'd like. I let him know that it would be great if Jay agrees. He tells me he's going to get off the phone and contact Jay. If he agrees, it will be arranged.

I don't talk to my parents for a few days. I hear from the Navy recruiter and everything is arranged. Jay and I will leave for Navy boot camp two weeks after we graduate high school. I decide to be trained as a radioman. They are needed on ships as well as on land. Seems like a good idea to me. The only thing left is parental approval since I'm only seventeen. When I get the forms, I give them to my mother. It only requires the signature of one parent. She smiles as she signs them.

My mother gives me back the signed paper and says, "What are you going to do with all your stuff you have here?"

"I don't know. I'm going to be going through Navy boot camp and then a few months of training. I won't have a place to put anything," I say.

"Maybe one of your friends could take your stuff."

"Yeah, maybe they could. I'll ask around."

"I am so glad you didn't go to jail before you graduated."

My feelings are hurt. I don't understand why but I tell myself my mother is being very realistic.

As I walk around school, I'm now among the group of kids who know what they will be doing after graduation. I learn there are also some guys going to the Army, Air Force, as well as Marines. Jay and I are the only ones going into the Navy.

My father isn't good at hiding his disappointment, but he comes around. A few weeks before graduation, he tells me he's glad I joined the Navy. He then asks me what I want to be done with all of my things while I'm in the Navy. I tell him I have no idea, but I'll keep asking my friends if they'll take them. Again, my feelings are hurt for some reason.

I'm experiencing a variety of emotions. I'm excited about leaving, but nervous about going into the military. There is sadness because I know I would have never been able to get into the college I wanted. I plan to continue with my writing. I keep telling myself joining the Navy is my best option. History seems to be repeating itself as my father joined the Army when he was only seventeen years old.

As my time for leaving approaches, I see a change in my parents. I think the reality that I will be gone begins to hit them. My mother starts being nice to me and doesn't get angry at things that would normally make her yell. I ask her why the change, and she tells me it doesn't matter anymore. My father is taking the time to come and talk with me. One Saturday, he comes back home after golf and doesn't go to the bar. He tells me he'd like to take me out for a meal. I agree, and we go to a nice place and have a great time. I'm treated to his stories about leaving for the Army and being in World War II as well as the Korean War. For the first time in my life, he shares stories about his childhood. It's a special time. I begin to feel I now know my father in a way I never did before.

My parents are being so nice to me, I don't know how to take it. I come down in the morning to make my breakfast and both my parents are sitting at the kitchen table. When I sit down, my mother says she's going to make me breakfast. I'm overwhelmed. My father then tells me they're going to give me a graduation party. I can invite anyone I want. I'm told my mother's oldest daughter and her family want to come to it. I don't know what to say. It doesn't seem real. I decide not to ask them why they are doing this because I don't want to think about it.

My senior year in high school is filled with being in the high school musical, being on the high school newspaper, and just enjoying my last year. The classes I take aren't too difficult. I'm able to spend plenty of time writing my stories. I get lots of form rejection letters as well as a few acceptances. There are yearbooks and the annual tradition of having people sign them. Some girls have tears in their eyes when they realize this will be our last year of yearbooks. We all begin to realize the end of our time in high school is coming soon.

On the day of my graduation from high school, things go well. The weather is nice and everyone is feeling happy. I take pictures with my parents, my friends, and their parents. All the graduating seniors from the high school newspaper get together for a picture. We even pose for pictures with some teachers. As I look back at the high school building, I realize whatever made me angry or upset when I was a student there no longer matters. It's over and won't ever upset me again. I tell myself I made it to the end.

A day or two later, my parents have the graduation party. I tell some people and hope for the best. I am stunned at the people who come to the party. Roger, Jay, and Neil all came to the party for a while. The man who was my scoutmaster when I was in Boy Scouts heard about the graduation party. He comes over to wish me well. The Navy recruiter also comes and spends some time at the party. There are a few neighbors who come to the party as well as some of my parents' friends.

I am stunned when I see the red hair and blue eyes of Tanya walking into the room. I can't believe it. Tanya comes over when she sees me and hugs me tightly. I'm so happy I can't say anything.

Tanya says, "Hey, I haven't heard from you for so long. A friend of my mother knows your father. When she said something about a graduation party, I had to come and say goodbye. I hope it's okay."

"Oh, it's great. I'm so happy you're here.

Tanya says, "You joined the Navy?"

"Yeah, what are you doing?"

"Nothing so exciting. Just going to college."

"That has to be exciting."

"Not this college."

We have a nice long talk. Before Tanya leaves, she gives me her address and tells me to write to her while I'm gone. I agree. Unfortunately, Tanya has a boyfriend. She does tell me if she ever feels she could ever handle having a worldly sailor boyfriend, she'll let me know.

The graduation party is wonderful. I think that good times like this could have happened for years and not just now. I think of negative things my parents have done but decide to let them go. This is the first party they've ever had for me. They're trying to be nice. I thank my parents and tell them how I appreciate all they've done for me. They both seem happy. It's almost like they're married.

My dad lets me have the car one day. I decide to drive around. As I move down through town, I see the crappy apartment where we lived. I see the bars my mother went to at night. I drive further and see the creek at the edge of town. I decide to keep driving. I then see a familiar building and stop. It's my old grade school. I look at the spot where I got into the fight with Billy. I leave there and before I know it, I'm driving past the auto repair garage that Billy's family owned. The building has changed and the business has a new name. I wonder what happened to Billy and his family, but realize I don't care.

I drive some more and take a turn down a rural road. Before I know it, I'm heading up toward the old farmhouse. I recognize a man who works with my father outside a house near there and stop to talk with him. I tell my father's friend about joining the Navy, and we share some stories about the past. I ask him about the old farmhouse. He tells me it's between residents. Nobody lives there right now.

I have an overwhelming urge to go and see the farmhouse. After talking with my father's friend, I drive there and stop in front of it. The farmhouse looks the same. The woods where I spent so much of my time seem to have been cut back a bit. I then notice the old stone building.

I quickly get out of the car and run to it. I go inside and it's filled with all sorts of junk. There are boards, rocks, old rusted tools, and all sorts of debris. I begin throwing things out of the way. It takes me a few minutes, but I see it. The canvas bag I had as a child. Tears stream down my face. I don't fight the urge to cry. I'm sobbing and thinking of the poor little boy who found a way to survive a horrible home life with this canvas bag. He was strong and brave. I'm proud of that little boy. I'm proud that he is me.

I carefully take the canvas bag. I lay it on the ground and open it up. The canvas is a mess. It's dirty, moldy, and has holes from rodents having chewed right through it. The blankets on the inside stink, and have rodent droppings all through them. It contains an old, rusted flashlight, rusted tin canteen, rusted cans of food, as well as decayed baseball magazines and books. Everything in it can be considered trash. To me, it is a treasure. I take it back to my father's car.

I have the canvas bag when I arrive home. It's put in a plastic bag. I then tightly seal the bag. I don't know what I'm going to do with it. The only thing I know for sure is I want it for now. It feels like I was able to reach into the past and pull out something from it. It's a few days before I can look at the plastic bag containing my canvas bag without getting emotional. I eventually stop and keep telling myself I never have to go back to that time in my life again.

The two weeks between my high school graduation and leaving for the Navy go by rather fast. Jay's family has a graduation party for him. They have everything with a Navy theme. Somebody gave an old sailor hat to Jay for him to wear at his party. There is a cake with a blue ocean and a ship with Jay's name on it on the icing. It is a great party.

We are both glad we can go to boot camp together. Jay and I spend a lot of time together talking about the future, being in the Navy, and realizing it is about to happen.

We agree to meet the Navy recruiter at a store parking lot about two blocks from my house the day we leave. On the day we leave, I'm trying to not give into my excitement or anxiety. That morning, there are pictures taken. One is taken of me holding a bumper sticker with the words *Go Navy* on it.

My father has to go to work that day. Before he leaves, he hugs me and says he's proud of me. Hugging my father is still awkward. I can sense his feelings for me. I don't know what to say. All I can do is thank him. I tell him I'll call as soon as possible. After my father leaves, I tell my mother I can walk up to meet the recruiter by myself. She insists on going with me.

When we get to the store parking lot, Jay is there with his mother and father. His mother's eyes are pink. I can tell his father is fighting back emotions. I don't know what to say to my mother. She doesn't look at me. It's as if my mother is uncomfortable, and I don't know what to do.

The recruiter pulls up in his car. Jay's mother is crying as she holds him, then his father hugs him. Neither seems as if they want to let him go.

I look at my mother and say, "Well, I guess this is it. I'll call you as soon as I can."

My mother says nothing. I look at her and I see sorrow, regret, and self-loathing. I have a sense she wants to tell me things about herself I don't know or understand. It seems as if she has just noticed me for the first time in my life. I know we should be emotional and hug one another. There should be tears between us. We do have the designation of son and mother in our relationship, but we have no real feelings for one another. There is an awkward silence between us. My mother then turns and starts walking back home. I get in the recruiter's car, and I'm ready to start my new life.

THE END

ABOUT THE AUTHOR

Lucas Kinkaid is the pen name of J. Michael Krivyanski. He is a syndicated columnist with Continental New Service. He has published hundreds of articles in print as well as online media. The author has published four books of his humor columns that previously appeared in various media. He has also written two Christian faith-based novels. *My Canvas Bag* is his first literary fiction novel. When not writing, he is busy biking, hiking and enjoying the outdoors with his wife.